nickelodeon
降世神通
AVATAR
THE LAST AIRBENDER

A Random House SCREEN COMIX™ Book

BOOK 1: WATER

VOLUME 1

Random House • New York

 Published in the United States by Random House Children's Books, a division of Penguin Random House LLC, 1745 Broadway, New York, NY, 10019, and in Canada by Penguin Random House Canada Limited, Toronto.

ISBN 978-0-593-37731-4
rhcbooks.com

Printed in the United States of America
10 9 8 7 6 5 4 3 2

CHAPTER ONE

THE BOY IN THE ICEBERG

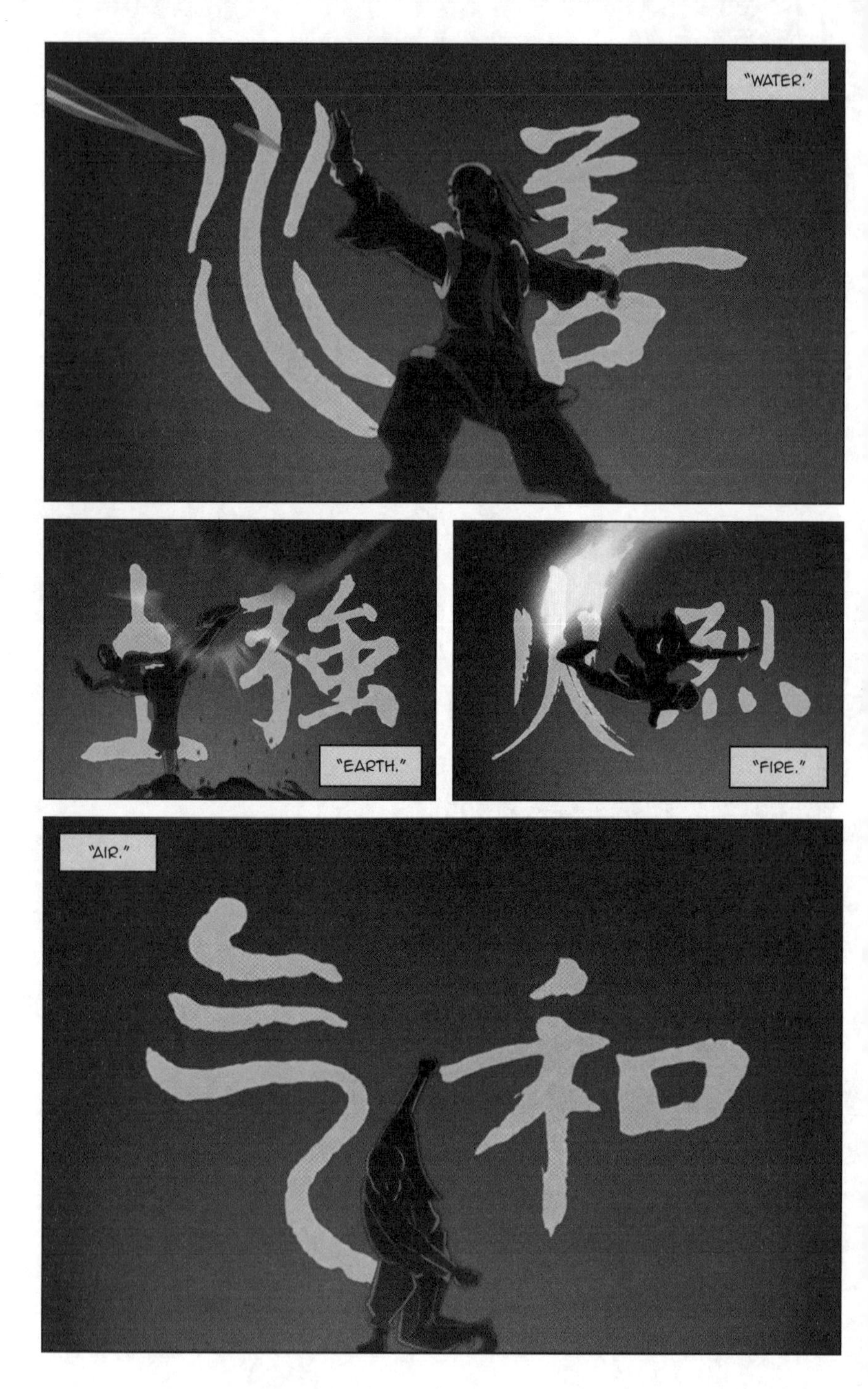
"WATER."
"EARTH."
"FIRE."
"AIR."

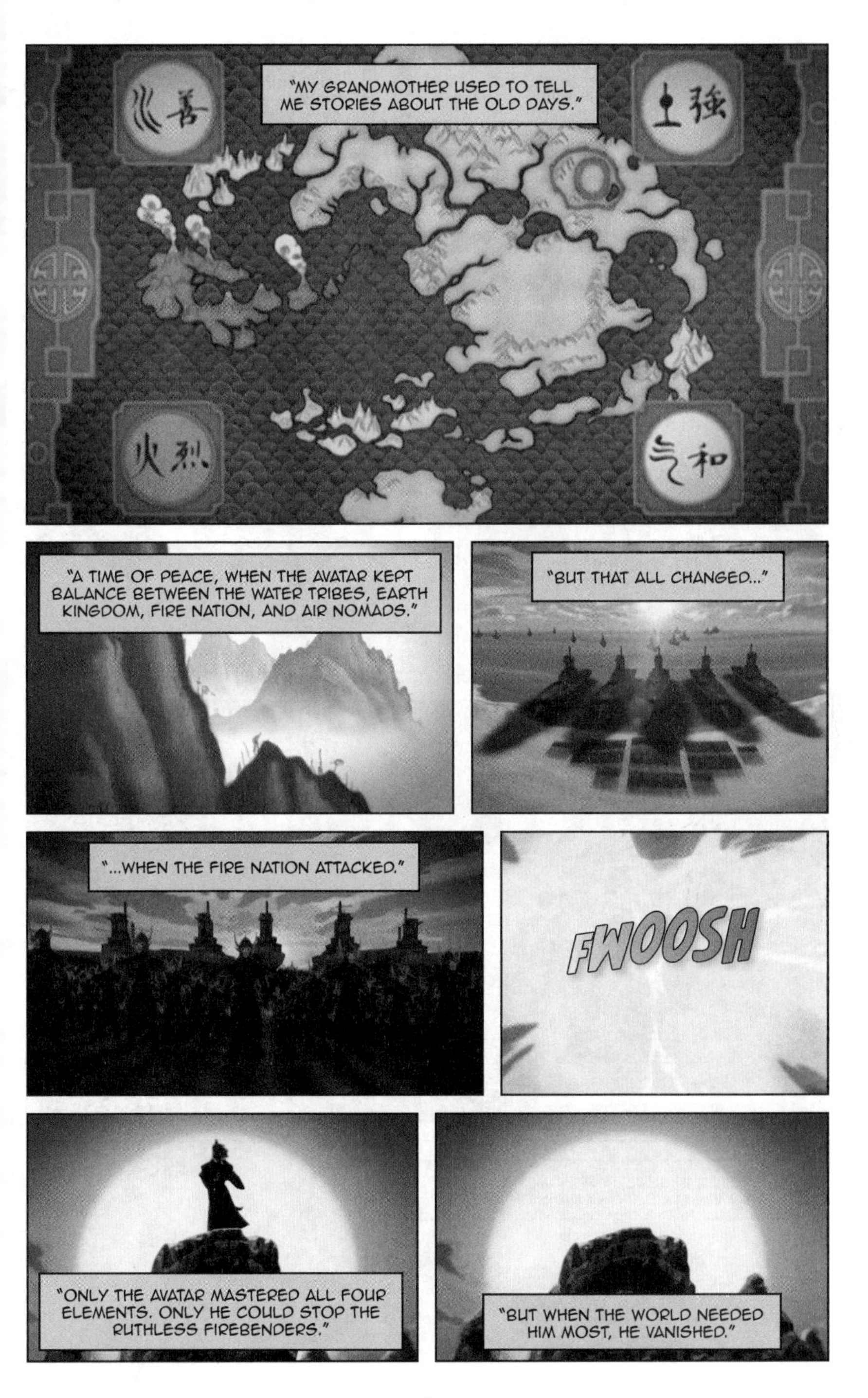
"MY GRANDMOTHER USED TO TELL ME STORIES ABOUT THE OLD DAYS."
"A TIME OF PEACE, WHEN THE AVATAR KEPT BALANCE BETWEEN THE WATER TRIBES, EARTH KINGDOM, FIRE NATION, AND AIR NOMADS."
"BUT THAT ALL CHANGED..."
"...WHEN THE FIRE NATION ATTACKED."
FWOOSH
"ONLY THE AVATAR MASTERED ALL FOUR ELEMENTS. ONLY HE COULD STOP THE RUTHLESS FIREBENDERS."
"BUT WHEN THE WORLD NEEDED HIM MOST, HE VANISHED."

"A HUNDRED YEARS HAVE PASSED, AND THE FIRE NATION IS NEARING VICTORY IN THE WAR."
"TWO YEARS AGO MY FATHER AND THE MEN OF MY TRIBE JOURNEYED TO THE EARTH KINGDOM TO HELP FIGHT AGAINST THE FIRE NATION..."
"...LEAVING ME AND MY BROTHER TO LOOK AFTER OUR TRIBE."
"SOME PEOPLE BELIEVE THAT THE AVATAR WAS NEVER REBORN INTO THE AIR NOMADS AND THAT THE CYCLE IS BROKEN..."
"BUT I HAVEN'T LOST HOPE."
"I STILL BELIEVE THAT SOMEHOW THE AVATAR WILL RETURN TO SAVE THE WORLD."

SOUTH SEA
IT'S NOT GETTING AWAY FROM ME THIS TIME.
WATCH AND LEARN, KATARA. THIS IS HOW YOU CATCH A FISH.

SOKKA... LOOK!
SPLOOSH
SHHH...KATARA, YOU'RE GONNA SCARE IT AWAY. MMM, I CAN ALREADY SMELL IT COOKIN'.
BUT, SOKKA...
I CAUGHT ONE!
HEY!
POP
SPLASH
AUGH!
SPLOOSH

WHY IS IT THAT EVERY TIME YOU PLAY WITH MAGIC WATER, I GET SOAKED?!
IT'S NOT MAGIC, IT'S WATERBENDING. AND IT'S...
YEAH, YEAH, AN "ANCIENT ART UNIQUE TO OUR CULTURE," BLAH, BLAH, BLAH.
LOOK, I'M JUST SAYING THAT IF I HAD WEIRD POWERS, I'D KEEP MY "WEIRDNESS" TO MYSELF.
YOU'RE CALLING ME WEIRD? I'M NOT THE ONE WHO MAKES MUSCLES AT MYSELF EVERY TIME I SEE MY REFLECTION IN THE WATER!

CRASH
HUFF HUFF
WATCH OUT!
GO LEFT!
GO LEFT!

AGH!
CRUNCH
YOU CALL THAT LEFT?!
YOU DON'T LIKE MY STEERING? WELL, MAYBE YOU SHOULD HAVE "WATERBENDED" US OUT OF THE ICE!
SO IT'S MY FAULT?
I KNEW I SHOULD HAVE LEFT YOU HOME.
LEAVE IT TO A GIRL TO SCREW THINGS UP!
YOU ARE THE MOST *SEXIST, IMMATURE, NUT-BRAINED--*

CRRAACKKK
I'M EMBARRASSED TO BE RELATED TO YOU!
CRRAACK
EVER SINCE MOM DIED, I'VE BEEN DOING ALL THE WORK AROUND CAMP WHILE YOU'VE BEEN OFF PLAYING SOLDIER!
PLOP PLOP
UH, KATARA--
I EVEN WASH ALL THE CLOTHES! HAVE YOU EVER SMELLED YOUR DIRTY SOCKS? LET ME TELL YOU...
CRRAACCKK
...NOT PLEASANT!
KATARA, SETTLE DOWN!

NO! THAT'S IT, I'M DONE HELPING YOU.
FROM NOW ON...
...YOU'RE ON YOUR OWN!
CRRAACKKK
CRRAACK
CREEEAAAK

SPLOOOOSHHH
WHOOSHH
YOU MEAN I DID THAT?
OKAY, YOU'VE GONE FROM WEIRD TO FREAKISH, KATARA...
YUP. CONGRATULATIONS.

FLOOSHHH
...

HE'S ALIVE! WE HAVE TO HELP!
KATARA, GET BACK HERE! WE DON'T KNOW WHAT THAT THING IS!

THUNK
FWOOSH
KABOOM

FIRE NATION NAVY SHIP
FINALLY.
UNCLE, DO YOU REALIZE WHAT THIS MEANS?
I WON'T GET TO FINISH MY GAME?
IT MEANS MY SEARCH...IT'S ABOUT TO COME TO AN END!

UGH.
THAT LIGHT CAME FROM AN INCREDIBLY POWERFUL SOURCE! IT HAS TO BE HIM!
OR IT'S JUST THE CELESTIAL LIGHTS! WE'VE BEEN DOWN THIS ROAD BEFORE, PRINCE ZUKO.
I DON'T WANT YOU TO GET TOO EXCITED OVER NOTHING. PLEASE--SIT. WHY DON'T YOU ENJOY A CUP OF CALMING JASMINE TEA.
I DON'T NEED ANY CALMING TEA! I NEED TO CAPTURE THE AVATAR!
HELMSMAN, HEAD A COURSE FOR THE LIGHT!

STOP!

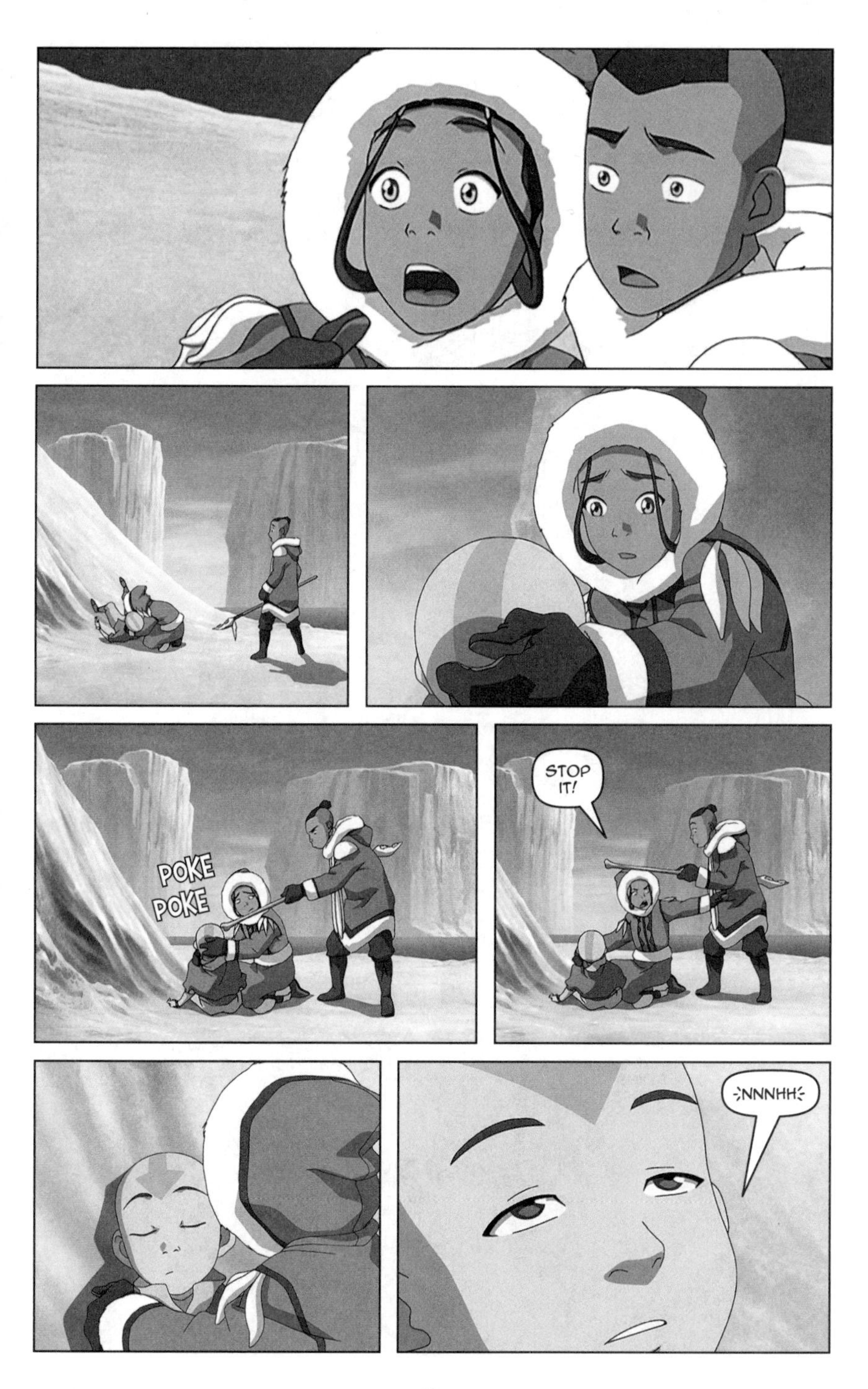
POKE
POKE
STOP IT!
NNNHH

I NEED TO ASK YOU SOMETHING...
PLEASE... COME CLOSER...
WHAT?
WHAT IS IT?
WILL YOU GO PENGUIN SLEDDING WITH ME?
UH...SURE... I GUESS...
WHAT'S GOING ON HERE?
YOU TELL US. HOW'D YOU GET IN THE ICE? AND WHY AREN'T YOU FROZEN?

I'M NOT SURE...
!
GRRRR
APPA! ARE YOU ALL RIGHT?
WAKE UP, BUDDY!

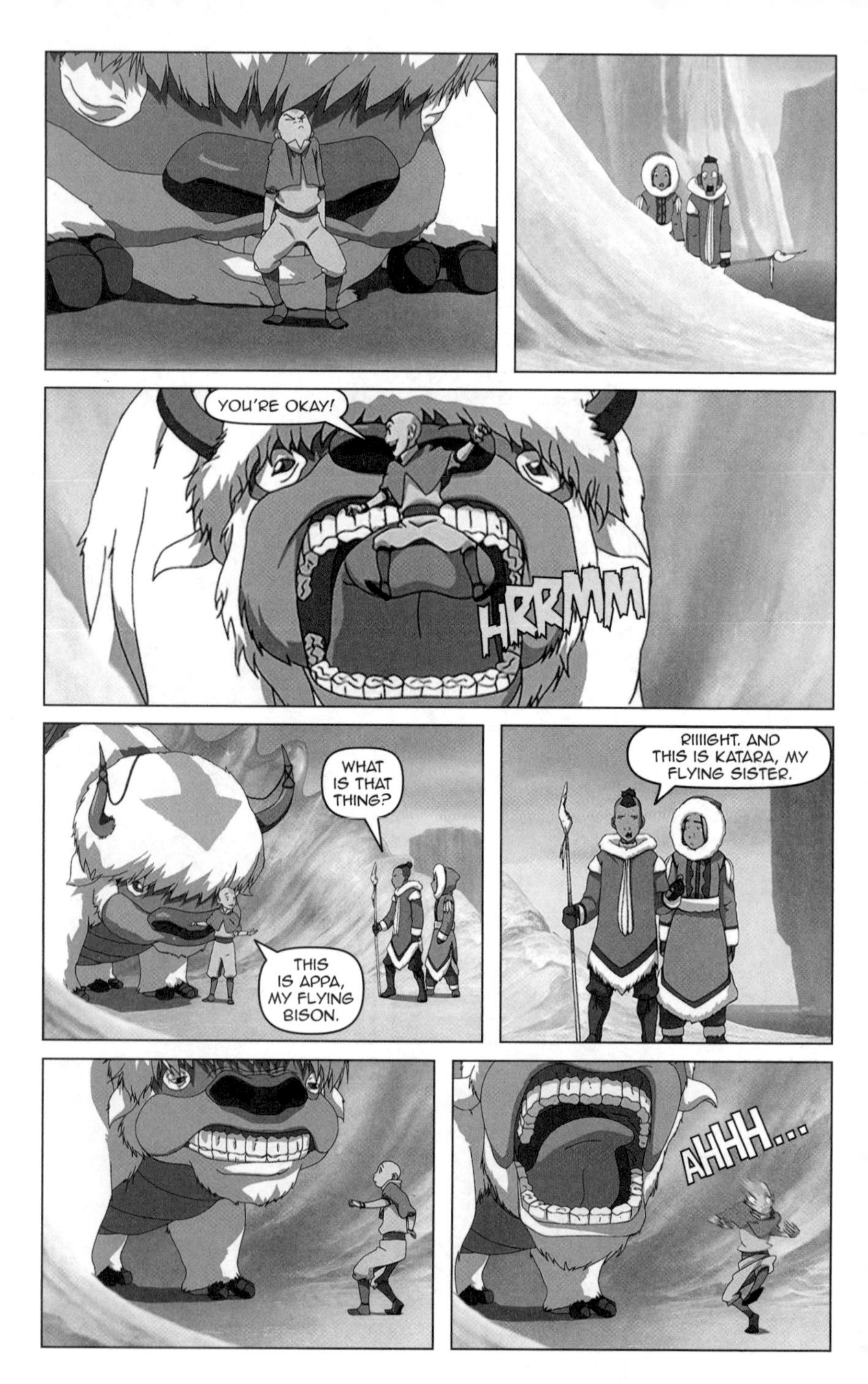
YOU'RE OKAY!
HRRMM
WHAT IS THAT THING?
THIS IS APPA, MY FLYING BISON.
RIIIIGHT. AND THIS IS KATARA, MY FLYING SISTER.
AHHH...

CHOOO
YECCHH!
DON'T WORRY, IT'LL WASH OUT.
BLECCHH.
SO, DO YOU GUYS LIVE AROUND HERE?
DON'T ANSWER THAT. DID YOU SEE THAT CRAZY BOLT OF LIGHT? HE WAS PROBABLY TRYING TO SIGNAL THE FIRE NAVY.
OH, YEAH, I'M SURE HE'S A SPY FOR THE FIRE NAVY--YOU CAN TELL BY THAT *EEEVIL* LOOK IN HIS EYE.

TWINKLE
THE PARANOID ONE IS MY BROTHER, SOKKA. YOU NEVER TOLD US YOUR NAME.
I'M AA--AAH... AAHHH...
...CHOOOO!

I'M AANG.
YOU JUST SNEEZED... AND FLEW TEN FEET IN THE AIR.
REALLY? IT FELT HIGHER THAN THAT.
YOU'RE AN AIRBENDER!
SURE AM!
GIANT LIGHT BEAMS, FLYING BISON, AIRBENDERS...I THINK I GOT MIDNIGHT SUN MADNESS.
I'M GOING HOME TO WHERE STUFF MAKES SENSE.

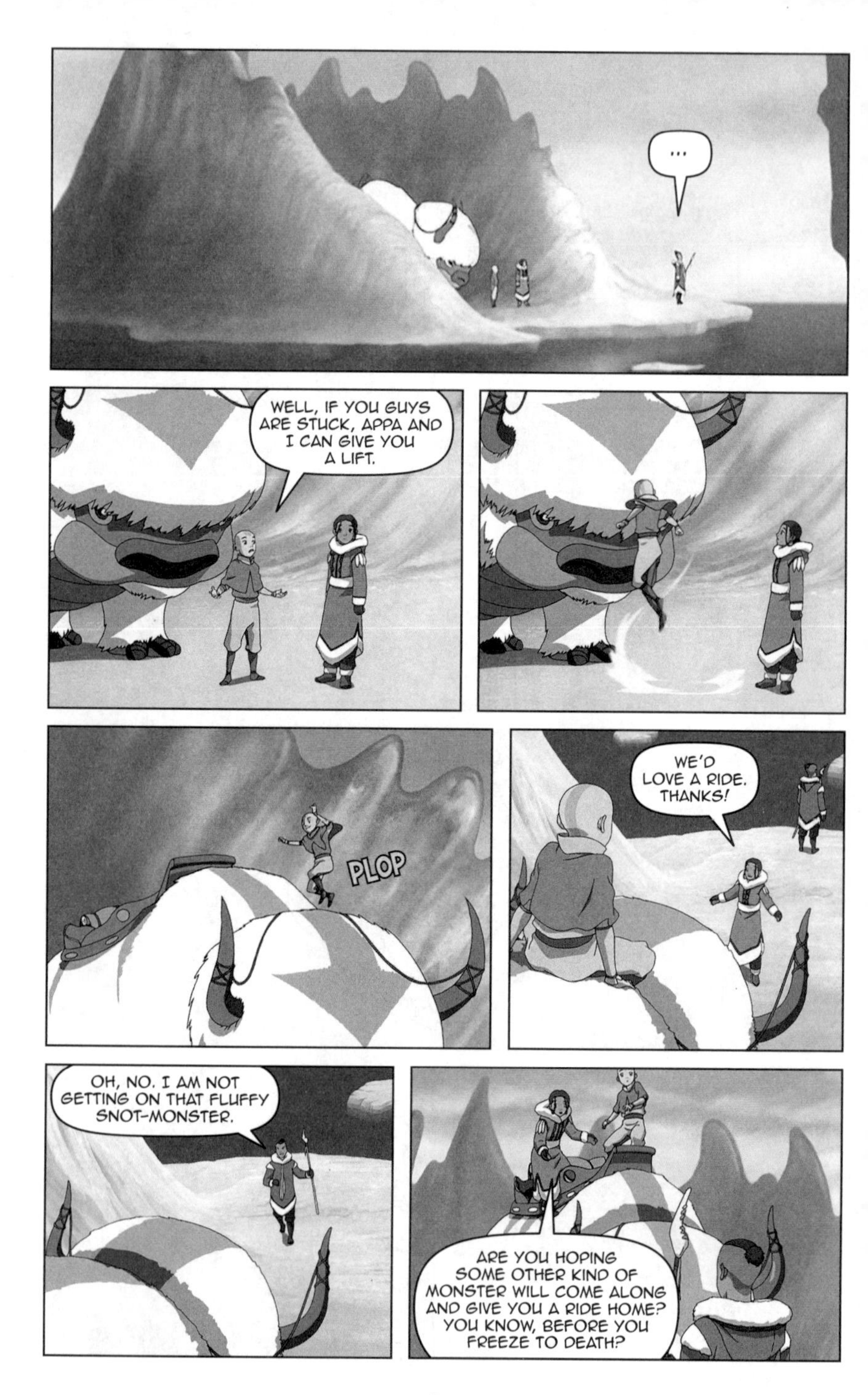
...
WELL, IF YOU GUYS ARE STUCK, APPA AND I CAN GIVE YOU A LIFT.
PLOP
WE'D LOVE A RIDE. THANKS!
OH, NO. I AM NOT GETTING ON THAT FLUFFY SNOT-MONSTER.
ARE YOU HOPING SOME OTHER KIND OF MONSTER WILL COME ALONG AND GIVE YOU A RIDE HOME? YOU KNOW, BEFORE YOU FREEZE TO DEATH?

OKAY. FIRST TIME FLIERS, HOLD ON TIGHT!
APPA, YIP-YIP!
SPLASH
COME ON, APPA, YIP-YIP.

WOW. THAT WAS TRULY AMAZING.
APPA'S JUST TIRED. A LITTLE REST AND HE'LL BE SOARING THROUGH THE SKY. YOU'LL SEE.
WHY ARE YOU SMILING AT ME LIKE THAT?
OH, I WAS SMILING?
BLECH.

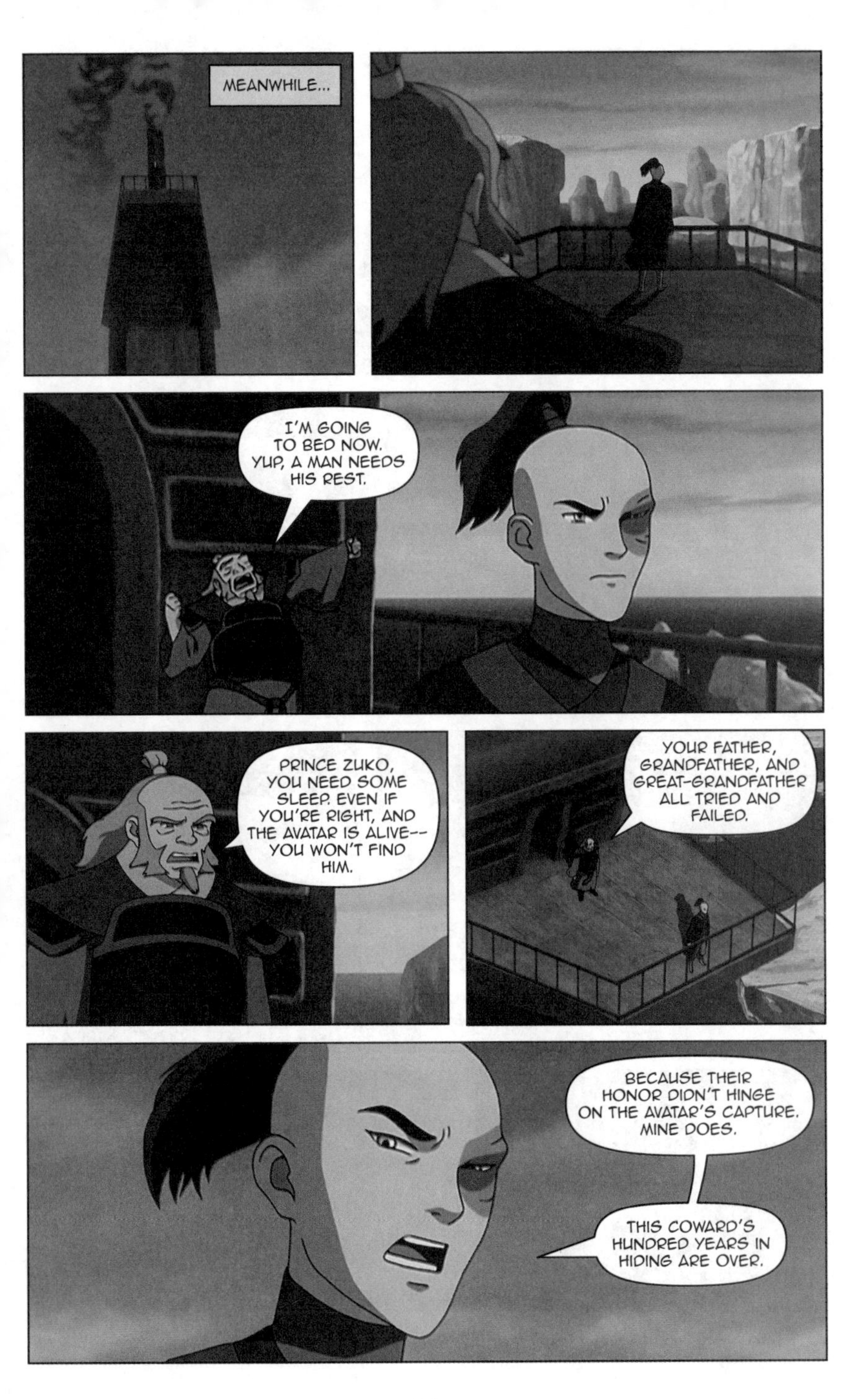
MEANWHILE...
I'M GOING TO BED NOW. YUP, A MAN NEEDS HIS REST.
PRINCE ZUKO, YOU NEED SOME SLEEP. EVEN IF YOU'RE RIGHT, AND THE AVATAR IS ALIVE-- YOU WON'T FIND HIM.
YOUR FATHER, GRANDFATHER, AND GREAT-GRANDFATHER ALL TRIED AND FAILED.
BECAUSE THEIR HONOR DIDN'T HINGE ON THE AVATAR'S CAPTURE. MINE DOES.
THIS COWARD'S HUNDRED YEARS IN HIDING ARE OVER.

HEY.
HEY, WHATCHA THINKING ABOUT?
I GUESS I WAS WONDERING-- YOUR BEING AN AIRBENDER AND ALL-- IF YOU HAD ANY IDEA WHAT HAPPENED TO THE AVATAR.
UH...NO, I DIDN'T KNOW HIM. I MEAN, I KNEW PEOPLE THAT KNEW HIM, BUT I DIDN'T. SORRY.
OKAY. JUST CURIOUS. GOOD NIGHT!
SLEEP TIGHT.

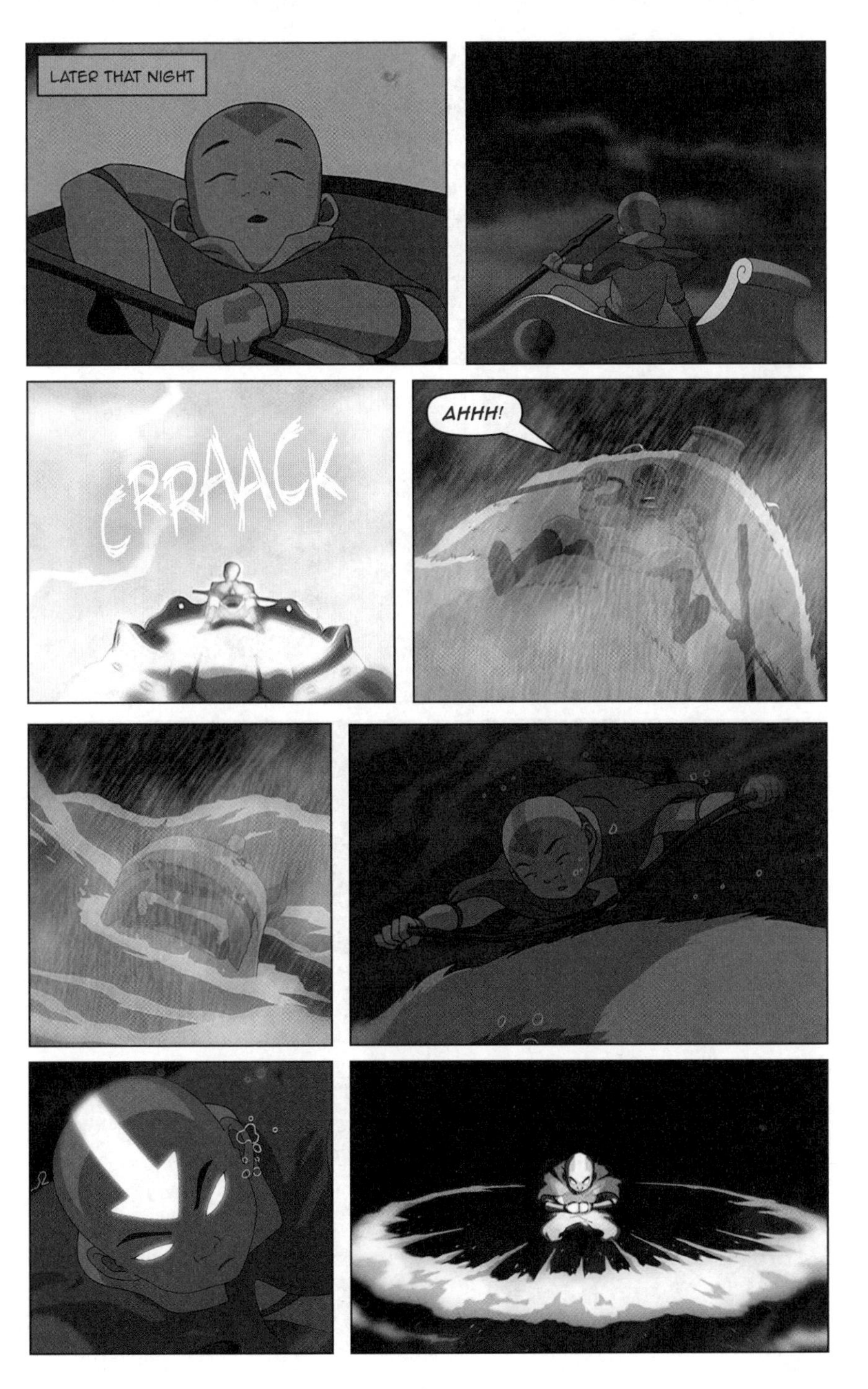
LATER THAT NIGHT
CRRAACK
AHHH!

"AANG! AANG, WAKE UP!"
-GASP-
IT'S OKAY. WE'RE IN THE VILLAGE NOW. COME ON, GET READY! EVERYONE'S WAITING TO MEET YOU!
-GASP-

WATER TRIBE VILLAGE
AANG, THIS IS THE... ENTIRE VILLAGE.
ENTIRE VILLAGE...AANG.
UH...WHY ARE THEY ALL LOOKING AT ME LIKE THAT? DID APPA SNEEZE ON ME?
WELL, NO ONE HAS SEEN AN AIRBENDER IN A HUNDRED YEARS.

WE THOUGHT THEY WERE EXTINCT...UNTIL MY GRANDDAUGHTER AND GRANDSON FOUND YOU.
EXTINCT...?
AANG, THIS IS MY GRANDMOTHER.
CALL ME GRAN-GRAN!
WHAT IS THIS, A WEAPON? YOU CAN'T STAB ANYTHING WITH THIS.
IT'S NOT FOR STABBING. IT'S FOR AIRBENDING.

WHUMP
MAGIC TRICK! DO IT AGAIN!
HAHAHA
NOT MAGIC--AIRBENDING. IT LETS ME CONTROL THE AIR CURRENTS AROUND MY GLIDER AND FLY.
YOU KNOW, LAST TIME I CHECKED, HUMANS CAN'T FLY.
CHECK AGAIN!
AHHHHHHHH

WHUMP
OOF!
...UUUGHH...
POP

MY WATCHTOWER!
THAT WAS AMAZING!
WHUMP
GREAT. YOU'RE AN AIRBENDER. KATARA'S A WATERBENDER. TOGETHER, YOU CAN JUST WASTE TIME ALL DAY LONG.
YOU'RE A WATERBENDER!

WELL, SORT OF... NOT YET...
ALL RIGHT, NO MORE PLAYING. COME ON, KATARA, YOU HAVE CHORES.
I TOLD YOU HE'S THE REAL THING, GRAN-GRAN! I'VE FINALLY FOUND A BENDER TO TEACH ME!
KATARA, TRY NOT TO PUT ALL YOUR HOPES IN THIS BOY.
BUT HE'S SPECIAL--I CAN TELL. I SENSE HE'S FILLED WITH MUCH WISDOM...
THEE? NOW MY TONGUE ITH THTUCK TO MY THTAFF!
HAHAHA!

MEANWHILE...
AGAIN.
WHOOSH

NO! POWER IN FIREBENDING COMES FROM THE BREATH, NOT THE MUSCLES.
THE BREATH BECOMES ENERGY IN THE BODY. THE ENERGY EXTENDS PAST YOUR LIMBS AND BECOMES...
...FIRE. GET IT RIGHT THIS TIME.
ENOUGH! I'VE BEEN DRILLING THIS SEQUENCE ALL DAY. TEACH ME THE NEXT SET. I'M MORE THAN READY.
NO. YOU'RE IMPATIENT. YOU HAVE YET TO MASTER YOUR BASICS. DRILL IT AGAIN.

THE SAGES TELL US THAT THE AVATAR IS THE LAST AIRBENDER. HE MUST BE OVER A HUNDRED YEARS OLD BY NOW. HE'S HAD A CENTURY TO MASTER THE FOUR ELEMENTS.
I'LL NEED MORE THAN BASIC FIREBENDING TO DEFEAT HIM.
YOU WILL TEACH ME THE ADVANCED SET!
VERY WELL. BUT FIRST...
I MUST FINISH MY ROAST DUCK.
MMMM!

NOW, MEN, IT'S IMPORTANT THAT YOU SHOW NO FEAR WHEN YOU FACE A FIREBENDER. IN THE WATER TRIBE, WE FIGHT TO THE LAST MAN STANDING!
FOR WITHOUT COURAGE, HOW CAN WE CALL OURSELVES MEN?
I GOTTA PEE.
LISTEN! UNTIL YOUR FATHERS RETURN FROM THE WAR, THEY'RE COUNTING ON YOU TO BE THE MEN OF THIS TRIBE.
AND THAT MEANS NO POTTY BREAKS!
BUT I REALLY GOTTA GO.
OKAY, WHO ELSE HAS TO GO?

HAVE YOU SEEN AANG?
GRAN-GRAN SAID HE DISAPPEARED OVER AN HOUR AGO.
WOW! EVERYTHING FREEZES IN THERE!
KATARA, GET HIM OUT OF HERE. THIS LESSON IS FOR WARRIORS ONLY.
WHEEEEEEEEEEEE!
FWUMP
STOP! STOP IT RIGHT NOW! WHAT'S WRONG WITH YOU? WE DON'T HAVE TIME FOR FUN AND GAMES WITH A WAR GOING ON.

WHAT WAR? WHAT ARE YOU TALKING ABOUT?
YOU'RE KIDDING, RIGHT?
PENGUIN!
ZZZZIPP
HE'S KIDDING, RIGHT?

AANG!
HEY, COME ON, LITTLE GUY. WANNA GO SLEDDING?
I HAVE A WAY WITH ANIMALS.
SQUAWK! SQUAWK!
AANG, I'LL HELP YOU CATCH A PENGUIN IF YOU TEACH ME WATERBENDING.
YOU GOT A DEAL! JUST ONE LITTLE PROBLEM-- I'M AN AIRBENDER, NOT A WATERBENDER.
ISN'T THERE SOMEONE IN YOUR TRIBE WHO CAN TEACH YOU?
NO. YOU'RE LOOKING AT THE ONLY WATERBENDER IN THE WHOLE SOUTH POLE.
THIS ISN'T RIGHT. A WATERBENDER NEEDS TO MASTER WATER. WHAT ABOUT THE NORTH POLE? THERE'S ANOTHER WATER TRIBE UP THERE, RIGHT? MAYBE THEY HAVE WATERBENDERS WHO COULD TEACH YOU.

MAYBE. BUT WE HAVEN'T HAD CONTACT WITH OUR SISTER TRIBE IN A LONG TIME. IT'S NOT EXACTLY "TURN RIGHT AT THE SECOND GLACIER"--IT'S ON THE OTHER SIDE OF THE WORLD!
BUT YOU FORGET, I HAVE A FLYING BISON. APPA AND I CAN PERSONALLY FLY YOU TO THE NORTH POLE.
KATARA, WE'RE GONNA FIND YOU A MASTER!
THAT'S...I MEAN, I DON'T KNOW...I'VE NEVER LEFT HOME BEFORE...
WELL, YOU THINK ABOUT IT. BUT IN THE MEANTIME, CAN YOU TEACH ME TO CATCH ONE OF THESE PENGUINS?
OKAY. LISTEN CLOSELY, MY YOUNG PUPIL. CATCHING PENGUINS IS AN ANCIENT AND SACRED ART.
OBSERVE.
PLOP
SQUAWK

WHOO!
HAHAHA!
WHOOSH
I HAVEN'T DONE THIS SINCE I WAS A KID!
YOU STILL ARE A KID!

WHOA...
WHAT IS THAT?
A FIRE NAVY SHIP. AND A VERY BAD MEMORY FOR MY PEOPLE.
AANG, STOP. WE'RE NOT ALLOWED TO GO NEAR IT.
THE SHIP COULD BE BOOBY-TRAPPED.
IF YOU WANT TO BE A BENDER, YOU HAVE TO LET GO OF FEAR.

THIS SHIP HAS HAUNTED MY TRIBE SINCE GRAN-GRAN WAS A LITTLE GIRL. IT WAS PART OF THE FIRE NATION'S FIRST ATTACKS.
OKAY, BACK UP. I HAVE FRIENDS ALL OVER THE WORLD, EVEN IN THE FIRE NATION. I'VE NEVER SEEN ANY WAR.

AANG, HOW LONG WERE YOU IN THAT ICEBERG?
I DON'T KNOW. A FEW DAYS, MAYBE?
I THINK IT WAS MORE LIKE A HUNDRED YEARS.
WHAT? THAT'S IMPOSSIBLE. DO I LOOK LIKE A 112-YEAR-OLD MAN TO YOU?
THINK ABOUT IT. THE WAR IS A CENTURY OLD. YOU DON'T KNOW ABOUT IT BECAUSE SOMEHOW, YOU WERE IN THERE THAT WHOLE TIME. IT'S THE ONLY EXPLANATION.
A HUNDRED YEARS...I CAN'T BELIEVE IT.
I'M SORRY, AANG. MAYBE SOMEHOW THERE'S A BRIGHT SIDE TO ALL THIS...
I DID GET TO MEET YOU.
COME ON, LET'S GET OUT OF HERE.

AANG, LET'S HEAD BACK. THIS PLACE IS CREEPY.
CREAK
SLAM
WHAT'S THAT YOU SAID ABOUT BOOBYTRAPS?
FSSHH
GASP!

FSSHH
KABOOM
UH-OH.

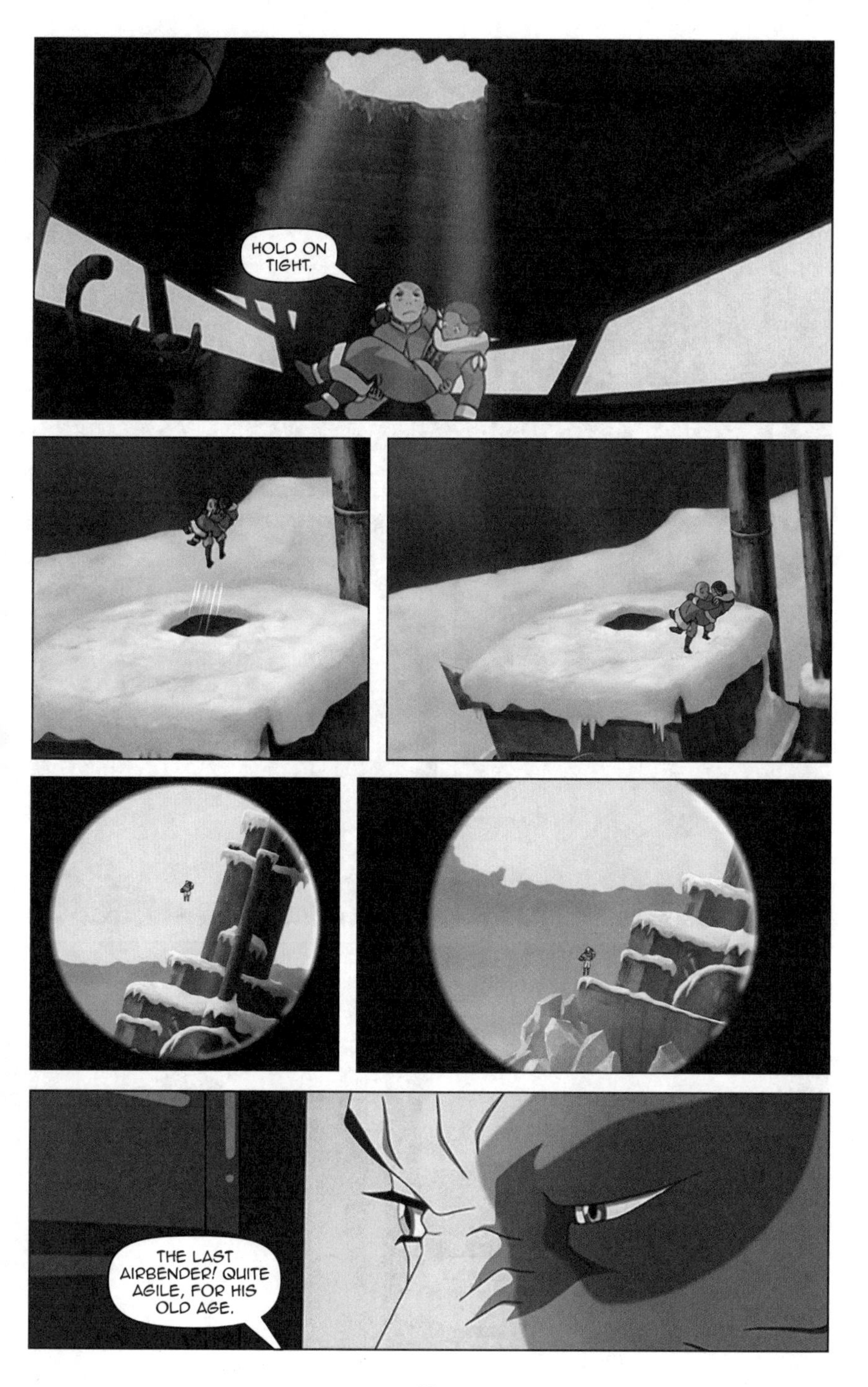
HOLD ON TIGHT.
THE LAST AIRBENDER! QUITE AGILE, FOR HIS OLD AGE.

WAKE MY UNCLE!
TELL HIM I'VE FOUND THE AVATAR.

AS WELL AS HIS HIDING PLACE!

CHAPTER TWO

THE AVATAR RETURNS

YAY! AANG'S BACK.
YAYYYY
I KNEW IT! YOU SIGNALED THE FIRE NAVY WITH THAT FLARE.
YOU'RE LEADING THEM STRAIGHT TO US, AREN'T YOU?
AANG DIDN'T DO ANYTHING. IT WAS AN ACCIDENT!

YEAH, WE WERE ON THE SHIP AND THERE WAS THIS BOOBYTRAP AND...WELL, WE BOOBIED RIGHT INTO IT.
KATARA, YOU SHOULDN'T HAVE GONE ON THAT SHIP. NOW WE COULD ALL BE IN DANGER!
DON'T BLAME KATARA... I BROUGHT HER THERE. IT'S MY FAULT.
AHA! THE TRAITOR CONFESSES!
WARRIORS, AWAY FROM THE ENEMY. THE FOREIGNER IS BANISHED FROM OUR VILLAGE.
SOKKA, YOU'RE MAKING A MISTAKE!
NO. I'M KEEPING MY PROMISE TO DAD. I'M PROTECTING YOU FROM THREATS LIKE HIM.

AANG IS NOT OUR ENEMY.
DON'T YOU SEE? AANG'S BROUGHT US SOMETHING WE HAVEN'T HAD IN A LONG TIME-- FUN.
FUN? WE CAN'T FIGHT FIREBENDERS WITH FUN.
YOU SHOULD TRY IT SOMETIME.
GET OUT OF OUR VILLAGE. NOW.
GRANDMOTHER, PLEASE. DON'T LET SOKKA DO THIS.
KATARA, YOU KNEW GOING ON THAT SHIP WAS FORBIDDEN. SOKKA IS RIGHT. I THINK IT BEST IF THE AIRBENDER LEAVES.

FINE. THEN I'M BANISHED, TOO!
COME ON, AANG. LET'S GO.
WHERE DO YOU THINK YOU'RE GOING?
TO FIND A WATERBENDER. AANG IS TAKING ME TO THE NORTH POLE.
I AM? GREAT!
KATARA, WOULD YOU REALLY CHOOSE HIM OVER YOUR TRIBE-- YOUR OWN FAMILY?
KATARA, I DON'T WANT TO COME BETWEEN YOU AND YOUR FAMILY.
SO YOU'RE LEAVING THE SOUTH POLE? THIS IS GOODBYE?

THANKS FOR PENGUIN SLEDDING WITH ME.
WHERE WILL YOU GO?
GUESS I'LL GO BACK HOME AND LOOK FOR THE AIRBENDERS.
WOW, I HAVEN'T CLEANED MY ROOM IN A HUNDRED YEARS. NOT LOOKING FORWARD TO THAT.
IT WAS NICE MEETING EVERYONE.
LET'S SEE YOUR BISON FLY NOW, AIRBOY.
COME ON, APPA. YOU CAN DO IT. YIP-YIP!
YEAH, I THOUGHT SO!

AANG, DON'T GO! I'LL MISS YOU!
I'LL MISS YOU, TOO.
COME ON, BOY.
KATARA, YOU'LL FEEL BETTER AFTER YOU--
YOU HAPPY NOW?! THERE GOES MY ONE CHANCE AT BECOMING A WATERBENDER.

ALL RIGHT, READY OUR DEFENSES! THE FIRE NATION COULD BE ON OUR SHORES ANY MOMENT NOW!
BUT I GOTTA--
AND NO POTTY BREAKS!

HRRRM
YEAH. I LIKED HER, TOO.
GASP!
RUMBLE
THE VILLAGE.
APPA, WAIT HERE!

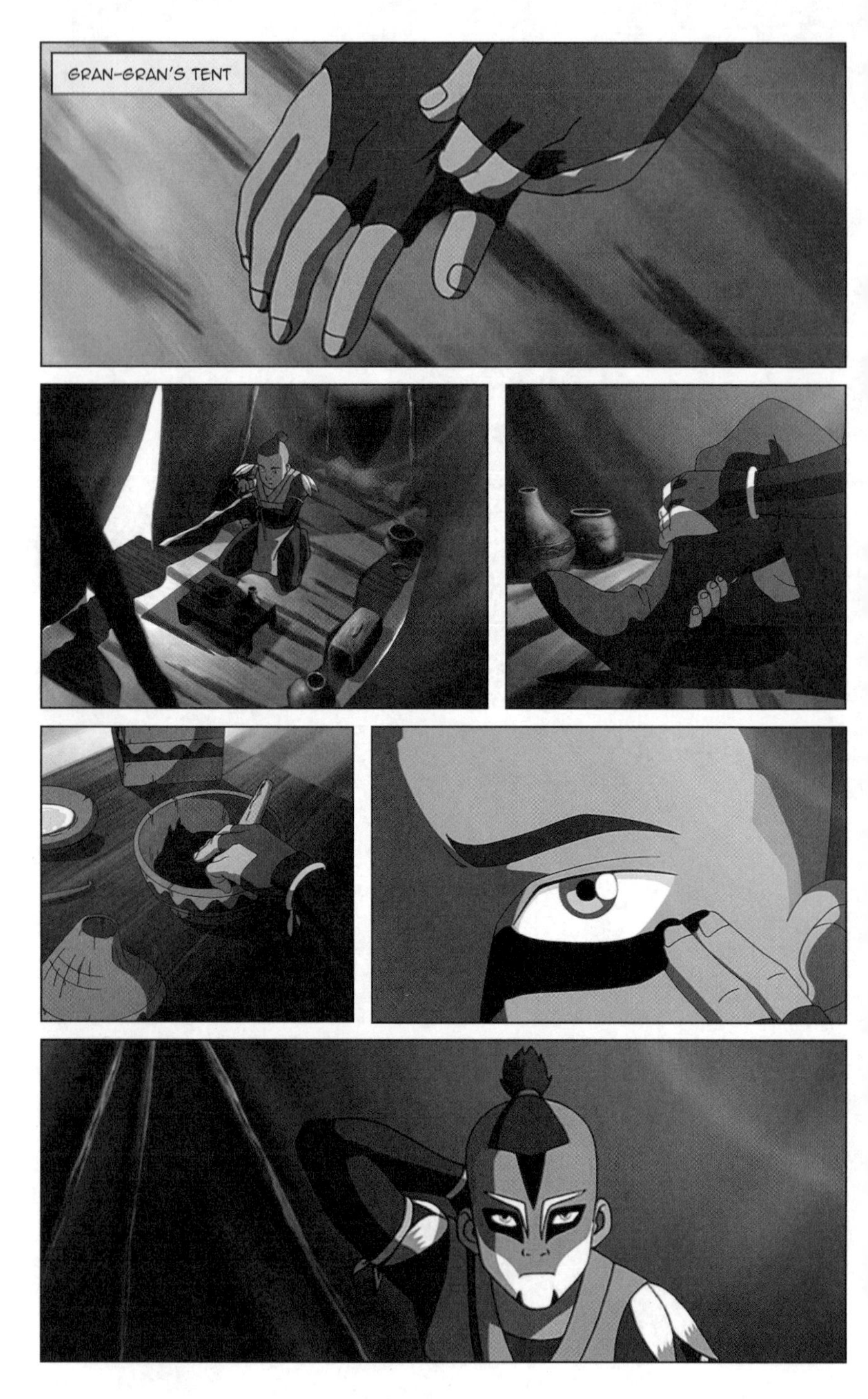
GRAN-GRAN'S TENT

ZUKO'S CHAMBERS

WATER TRIBE VILLAGE
RUMBLE
RUMBLE

RUMBLE
OH, MAN.
RUMBLE RUMBLE
OH, MAN.
CRUNCH

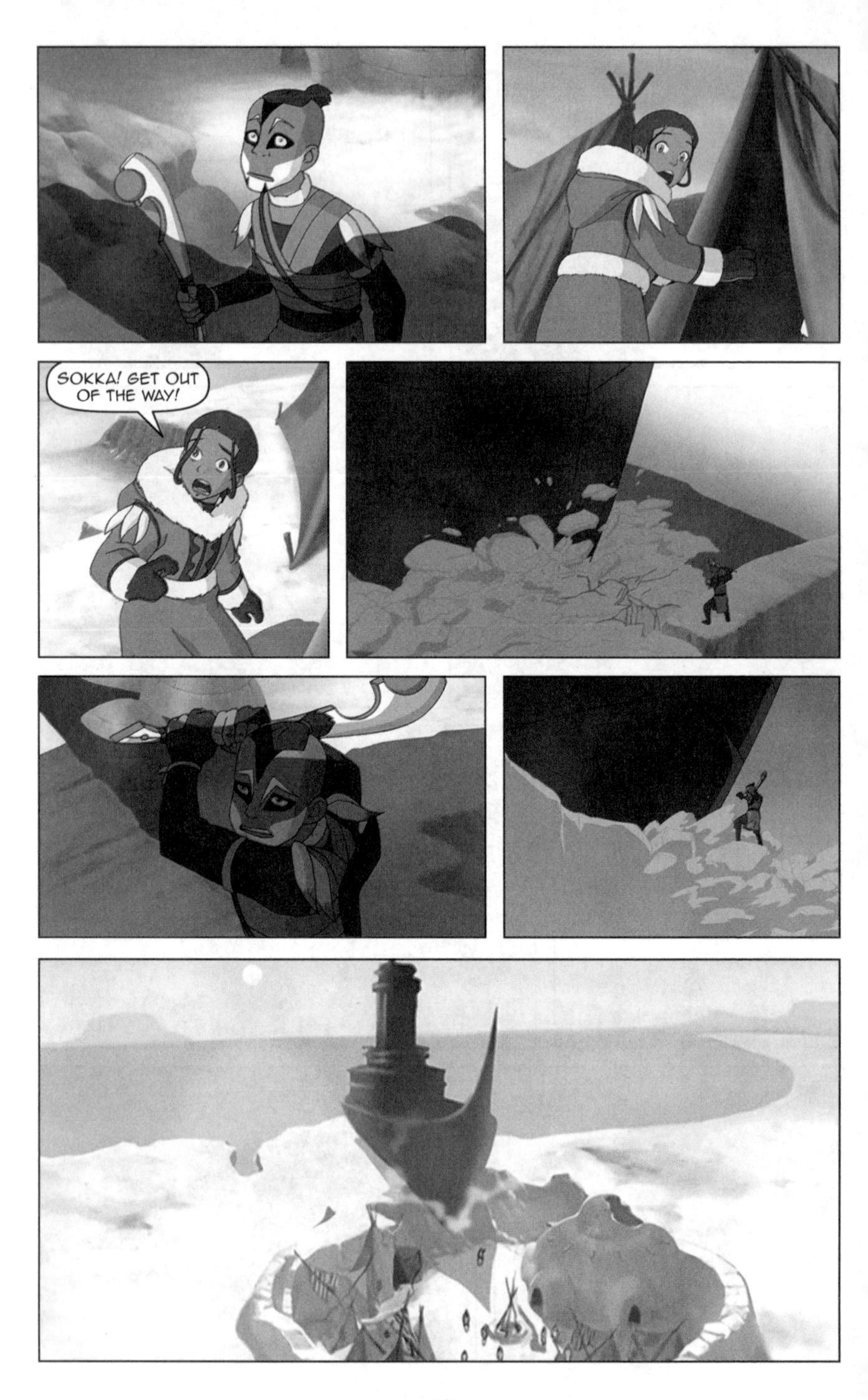
SOKKA! GET OUT
OF THE WAY!

PPPSSHHHHH
THWUMP

AHHHH!
AHHHH!
FWUMP
THUD

WHERE ARE YOU HIDING HIM?
HE'D BE ABOUT THIS AGE? MASTER OF ALL ELEMENTS?
FWOOSH
AGHHH
I KNOW YOU'RE HIDING HIM!

AHHHH!
SHOW NO FEAR!

?!
ZZZZIPP

SLAM
BOK
HEY, KATARA. HEY, SOKKA.
HI, AANG. THANKS FOR COMING.

WHOOOSH
LOOKING FOR ME?
YOU'RE THE AIRBENDER? YOU'RE THE AVATAR?
AANG?
NO WAY...

I'VE SPENT YEARS PREPARING FOR THIS ENCOUNTER. TRAINING. MEDITATING. YOU'RE JUST A CHILD!
WELL, YOU'RE JUST A TEENAGER.
FWOOSH
TAK
TAK
TAK
FWOOSH
AGHHH

IF I GO WITH YOU, WILL YOU PROMISE TO LEAVE EVERYONE ALONE?
NO, AANG! DON'T DO THIS.
DON'T WORRY, KATARA. IT'LL BE OKAY.

TAKE CARE OF APPA FOR ME UNTIL I GET BACK!
HEAD A COURSE TO THE FIRE NATION. I'M GOING HOME!
PPPSSHHHHH

WE HAVE TO GO AFTER THAT SHIP, SOKKA. AANG SAVED OUR TRIBE. NOW WE HAVE TO SAVE HIM.
KATARA, I--
WHY CAN'T YOU REALIZE THAT HE'S ON OUR SIDE?

IF WE DON'T HELP HIM, NO ONE WILL. I KNOW YOU DON'T LIKE AANG, BUT WE OWE HIM AND--
ARE YOU GONNA TALK ALL DAY, OR ARE YOU COMING WITH ME?
SOKKA!
GET IN. WE'RE GOING TO SAVE YOUR BOYFRIEND.
HE'S NOT MY--
WHATEVER.
WHAT DO YOU TWO THINK YOU'RE DOING?
YOU'LL NEED THESE. YOU HAVE A LONG JOURNEY AHEAD OF YOU.

IT'S BEEN SO LONG SINCE I'VE HAD HOPE. BUT YOU BROUGHT IT BACK TO LIFE, MY LITTLE WATERBENDER.
AND YOU, MY BRAVE WARRIOR. BE NICE TO YOUR SISTER.
YEAH. OKAY, GRAN.
AANG IS THE AVATAR. HE'S THE WORLD'S ONLY CHANCE. YOU BOTH FOUND HIM FOR A REASON. NOW YOUR DESTINIES ARE INTERTWINED WITH HIS.
THERE'S NO WAY WE'RE GOING TO CATCH A WARSHIP WITH A CANOE.
HRRRRM
APPA!
YOU JUST LOVE TAKING ME OUT OF MY COMFORT ZONE, DON'T YOU?

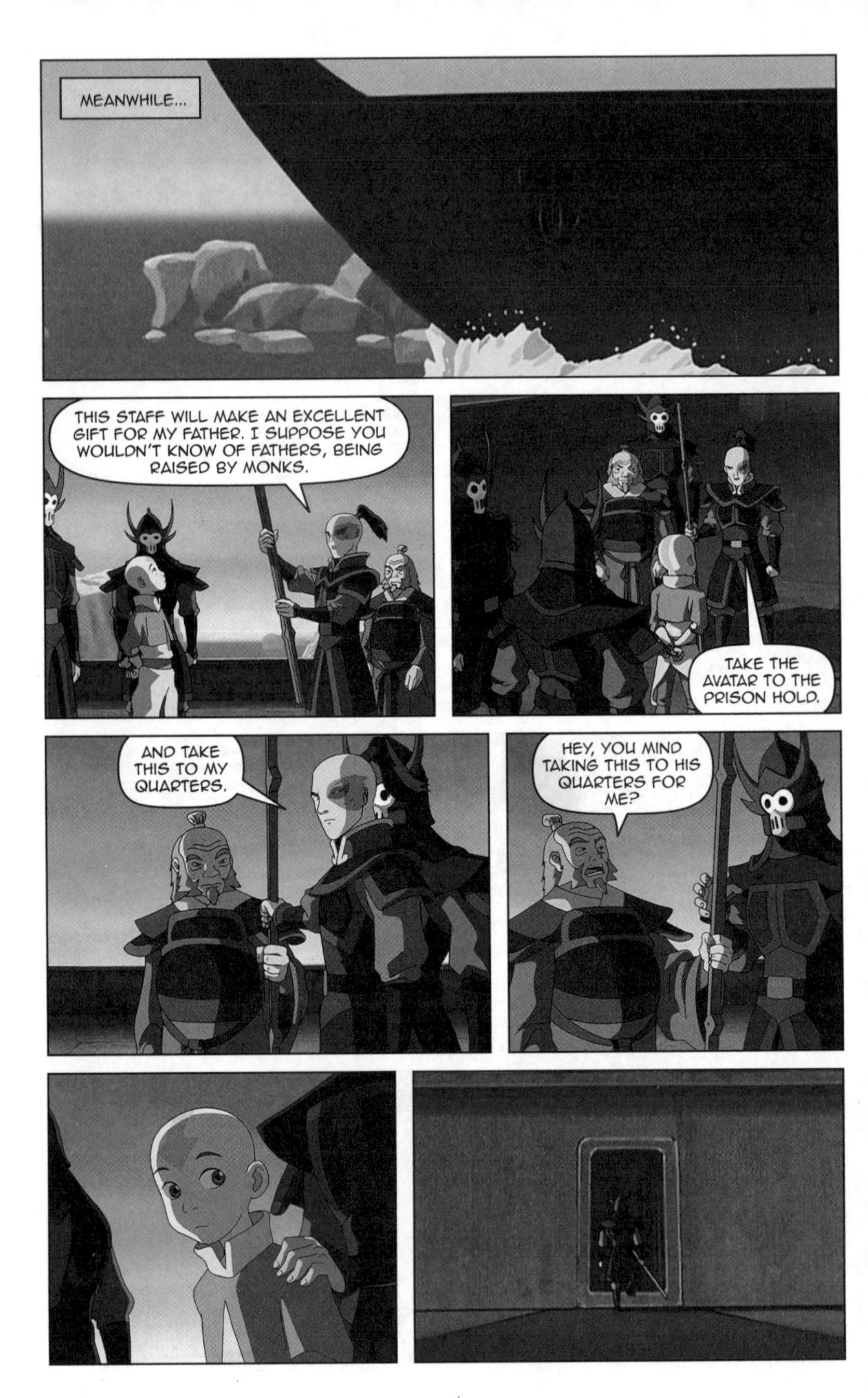
MEANWHILE...
THIS STAFF WILL MAKE AN EXCELLENT GIFT FOR MY FATHER. I SUPPOSE YOU WOULDN'T KNOW OF FATHERS, BEING RAISED BY MONKS.
TAKE THE AVATAR TO THE PRISON HOLD.
AND TAKE THIS TO MY QUARTERS.
HEY, YOU MIND TAKING THIS TO HIS QUARTERS FOR ME?

SO...I GUESS YOU'VE NEVER FOUGHT AN AIRBENDER BEFORE.
I BET I COULD TAKE YOU BOTH WITH MY HANDS TIED BEHIND MY BACK.
SILENCE.
HHHAAA
HHHAAA

WHHOOOSSSHH
WHAM
WHAM

WHOOSH
CREEAKK
PANT
PANT
THE AVATAR HAS ESCAPED!

SOUTH SEA
GO. FLY. SOAR.
PLEASE, APPA. WE NEED YOUR HELP. AANG NEEDS YOUR HELP...
UP. ASCEND. ELEVATE.
SOKKA DOESN'T BELIEVE YOU CAN FLY, BUT I DO, APPA. COME ON, DON'T YOU WANT TO SAVE AANG?
HRRRMMM

WHAT WAS IT THAT KID SAID? YEE-HA. HUP-HUP. WA-HOO.
YIP-YIP?
HRRRMMM
HRRMM
HE'S FLYING! HE'S FLYING! KATARA, HE'S--
I MEAN, BIG DEAL. HE'S FLYING.

AHHH!
PRINCE ZUKO'S SHIP
YOU HAVEN'T SEEN MY STAFF AROUND, HAVE YOU?
WHOOSH
THANKS ANYWAY!

FWOOOSH
FFFT
SNORE

SORRY!
MY STAFF!
LOOKS LIKE I UNDERESTIMATED YOU.
SLAM
FWOOSH

FWOOSH
UGH!

NGH!
FOOM
WHAP
SLAM
...GROAN...

WHOOSH

WHUMP

NAARGGHH!

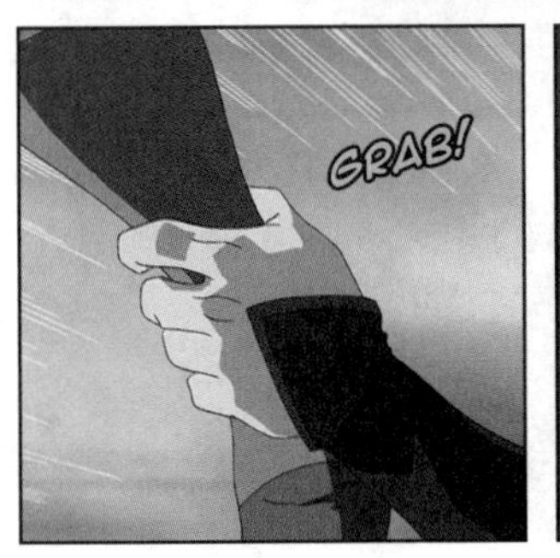
GRAB!

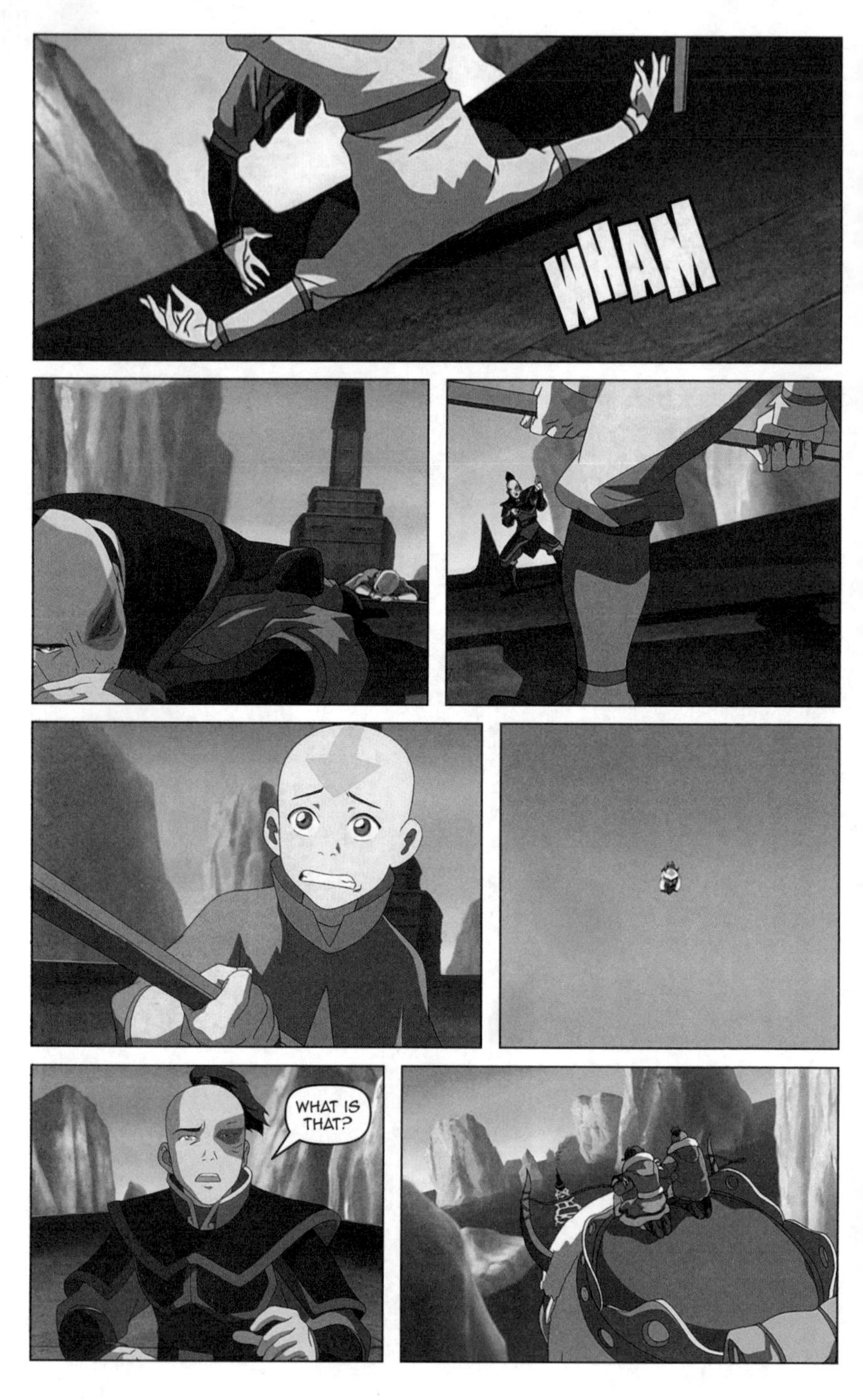
WHAM
WHAT IS THAT?

APPA!
FOOM
FWOOSH
WH-WHOA...
SPLASH

AANG! NO!
AANG!

SPLOOSH

AHHH!

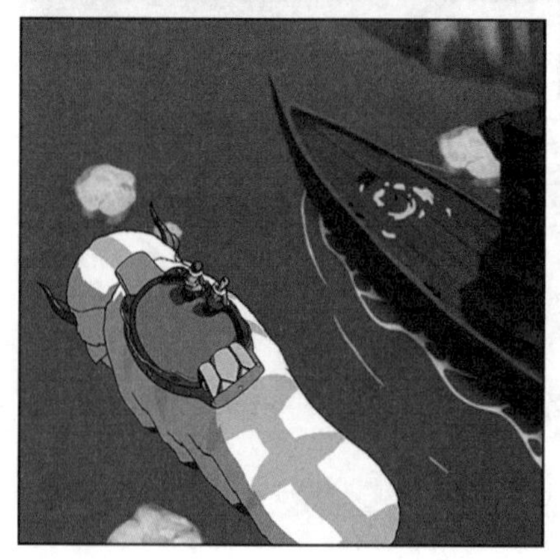

DID YOU SEE WHAT HE JUST DID?!
NOW THAT WAS SOME WATERBENDING.

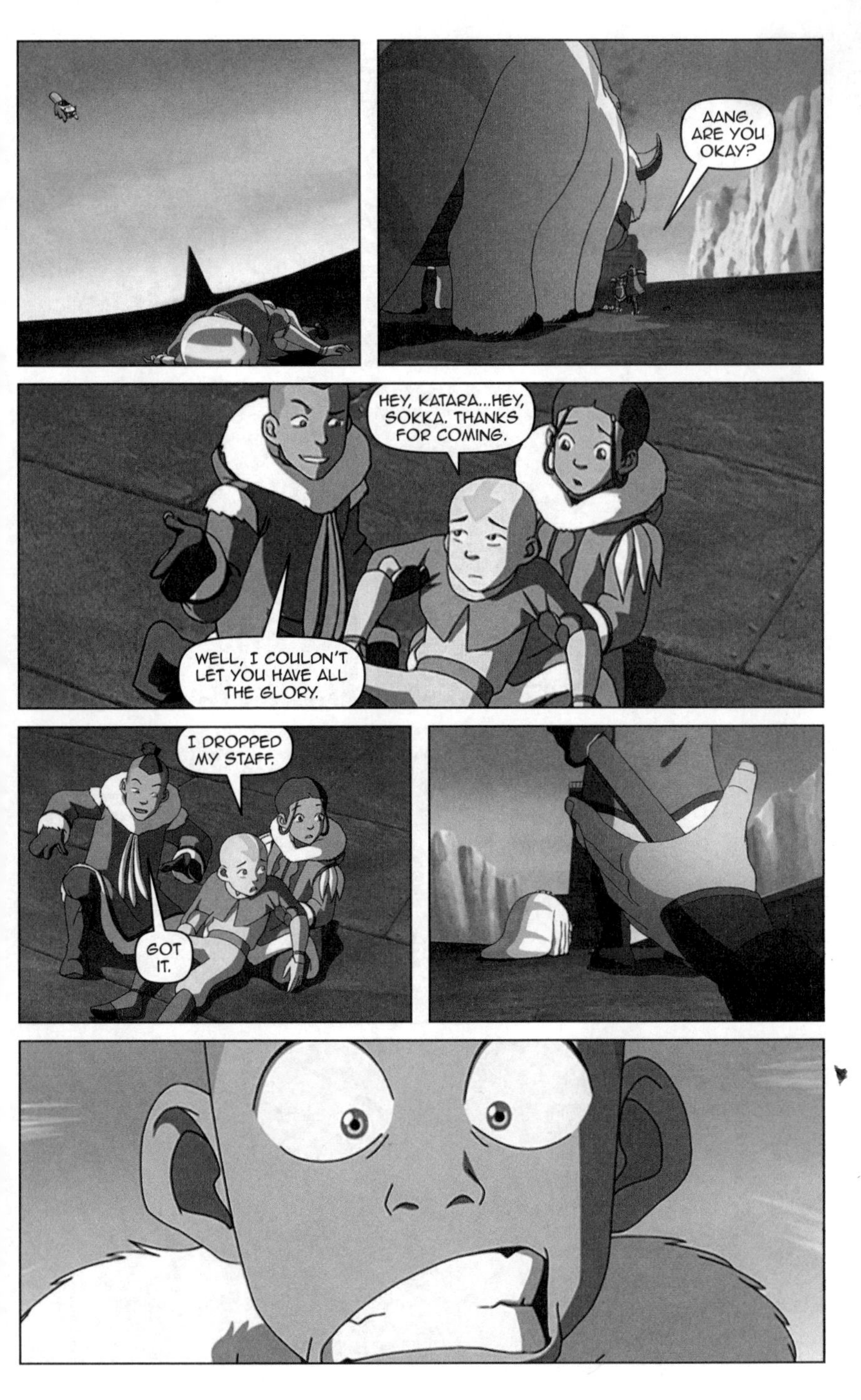
AANG, ARE YOU OKAY?
HEY, KATARA...HEY, SOKKA. THANKS FOR COMING.
WELL, I COULDN'T LET YOU HAVE ALL THE GLORY.
I DROPPED MY STAFF.
GOT IT.

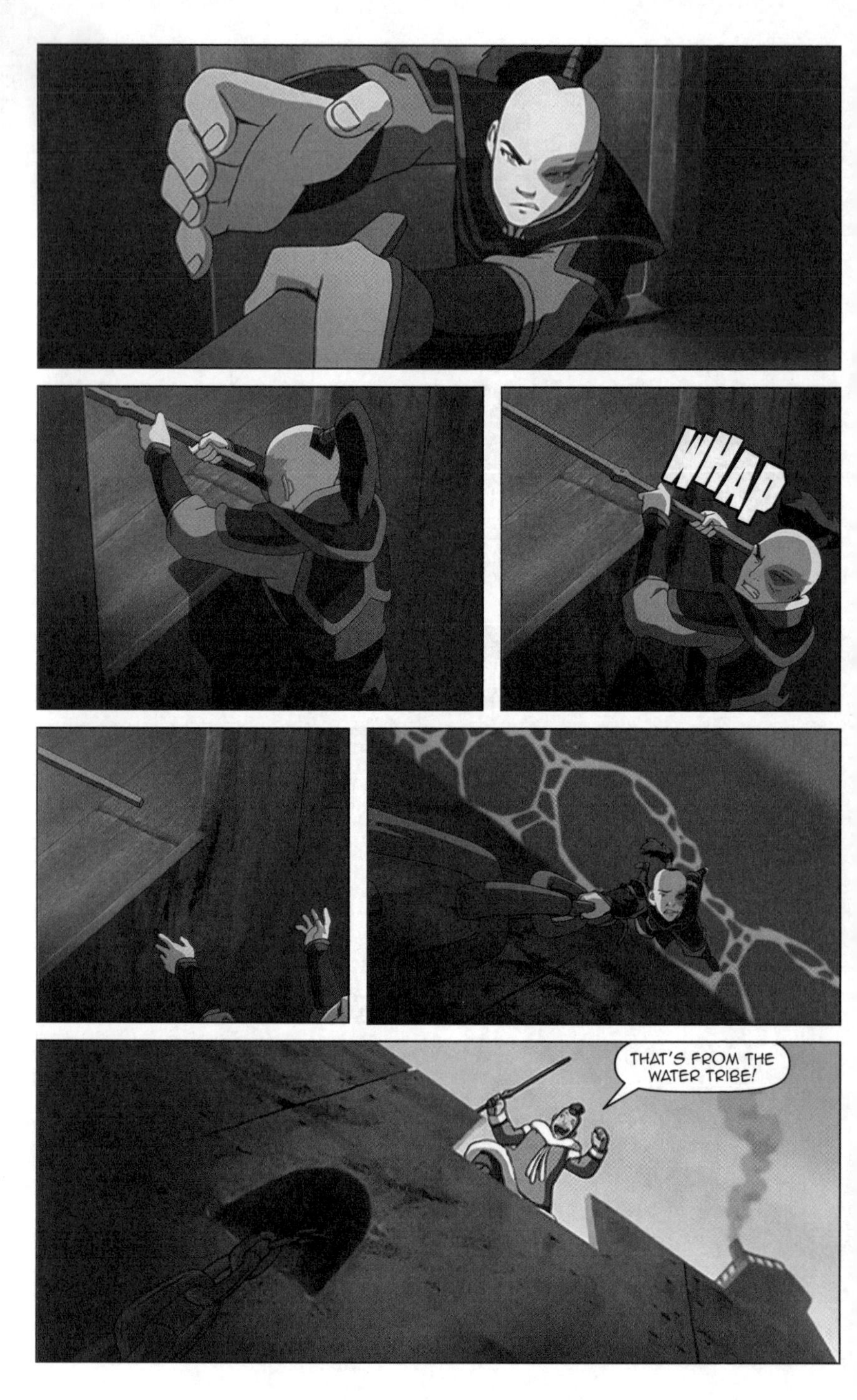
WHAP
THAT'S FROM THE WATER TRIBE!

HWAUH!

KATARA!
FREEZE

HURRY UP, SOKKA!
I'M JUST A GUY WITH A BOOMERANG. I DIDN'T ASK FOR ALL THIS FLYING AND MAGIC...
CHOK
CHOK
YIP-YIP! YIP-YIP!

SHOOT THEM DOWN!
FWOOSH

WHUMP
HAHAHA

GOOD NEWS FOR THE FIRE LORD. THE FIRE NATION'S GREATEST THREAT-- IS JUST A LITTLE KID!
THAT "KID," UNCLE--JUST DID THIS. I WON'T UNDERESTIMATE HIM AGAIN.
DIG THE SHIP OUT AND FOLLOW THEM!
FSSS
FSSS
FSSS
...UH...AS SOON AS YOU'RE DONE WITH THAT.

HOW DID YOU DO THAT? WITH THE WATER! IT WAS THE MOST AMAZING THING I'VE EVER SEEN!
I DON'T KNOW. I JUST SORT OF... DID IT.
WHY DIDN'T YOU TELL US YOU WERE THE AVATAR?
BECAUSE... I NEVER WANTED TO BE.
BUT, AANG, THE WORLD'S BEEN WAITING FOR THE AVATAR TO RETURN AND FINALLY PUT AN END TO THIS WAR.
AND HOW AM I GOING TO DO THAT?

ACCORDING TO LEGEND, YOU NEED TO FIRST MASTER WATER, THEN EARTH, THEN FIRE, RIGHT?
THAT'S WHAT THE MONKS TOLD ME.
WELL, IF WE GO TO THE NORTH POLE, YOU CAN MASTER WATERBENDING.
WE COULD LEARN IT TOGETHER!
AND, SOKKA, I'M SURE YOU'LL GET TO KNOCK SOME FIREBENDER HEADS ON THE WAY.
I'D LIKE THAT. I'D REALLY LIKE THAT.
THEN WE'RE IN THIS TOGETHER!

ALL RIGHT, BUT BEFORE I LEARN WATERBENDING, WE HAVE SOME SERIOUS BUSINESS TO ATTEND TO...
HERE, HERE, AND HERE.
WHAT'S THERE?
HERE, WE'LL RIDE THE HOPPING LLAMAS, THEN WAY OVER HERE WE'LL SURF ON THE BACKS OF GIANT KOI FISH.
THEN BACK OVER HERE WE'LL RIDE THE HOG MONKEYS. THEY DON'T LIKE PEOPLE RIDING THEM...
BUT THAT'S WHAT MAKES IT FUN.

CHAPTER THREE

THE SOUTHERN AIR TEMPLE

EARTH NATION
WAIT TILL YOU SEE IT, KATARA. THE AIR TEMPLE IS ONE OF THE MOST BEAUTIFUL PLACES IN THE WORLD!
AANG, I KNOW YOU'RE EXCITED, BUT IT'S BEEN A HUNDRED YEARS SINCE YOU'VE BEEN HOME.
THAT'S WHY I'M SO EXCITED.
IT'S JUST THAT A LOT CAN CHANGE IN ALL THAT TIME.
I KNOW, BUT I NEED TO SEE IT FOR MYSELF.
FWUP
ZZZZ

WAKE UP, SOKKA! AIR TEMPLE, HERE WE COME!
SLEEP NOW. TEMPLE LATER.
SOKKA, WAKE UP! THERE'S A PRICKLESNAKE IN YOUR SLEEPING BAG!
AHH!
GET IT OFF, GET IT OFF!
GREAT, YOU'RE AWAKE. LET'S GO!

EARTH NATION HARBOR
UNCLE, I WANT THE REPAIRS MADE AS QUICKLY AS POSSIBLE. I DON'T WANT TO STAY TOO LONG AND RISK LOSING HIS TRAIL.
YOU MEAN THE AVATAR?
DON'T MENTION HIM ON THESE DOCKS. ONCE WORD GETS OUT THAT HE IS ALIVE, EVERY FIREBENDER WILL BE OUT LOOKING FOR HIM. AND I DON'T WANT ANYONE GETTING IN THE WAY.
GETTING IN THE WAY OF WHAT, PRINCE ZUKO?
CAPTAIN ZHAO.

IT'S COMMANDER NOW.
AND GENERAL IROH...GREAT HERO OF OUR NATION!
RETIRED GENERAL.
THE FIRE LORD'S BROTHER AND SON ARE WELCOME GUESTS ANYTIME. WHAT BRINGS YOU TO MY HARBOR?
OUR SHIP IS BEING REPAIRED.
THAT'S QUITE A BIT OF DAMAGE.
YES, YOU WOULDN'T BELIEVE WHAT HAPPENED. UNCLE, TELL COMMANDER ZHAO WHAT HAPPENED.
YES, I WILL DO THAT. IT WAS INCREDIBLE!
WHAT, DID WE CRASH OR SOMETHING?
YES. RIGHT INTO AN EARTH KINGDOM SHIP.

REALLY? YOU MUST REGALE ME WITH ALL THE THRILLING DETAILS. JOIN ME FOR A DRINK?
SORRY, BUT WE HAVE TO GO--
PRINCE ZUKO, SHOW COMMANDER ZHAO YOUR RESPECT.
WE WOULD BE HONORED TO JOIN YOU. DO YOU HAVE ANY GINSENG TEA? IT'S MY FAVORITE.

PATOLA MOUNTAIN RANGE
RUMBLE
HEY, STOMACH, BE QUIET, ALL RIGHT? I'M TRYING TO FIND US SOME FOOD.
HEY, WHO ATE ALL MY BLUBBERED SEAL JERKY?
OH. THAT WAS FOOD? I USED IT TO START THE CAMPFIRE LAST NIGHT. SORRY!

YOU WHAT?! AWWW, NO WONDER THE FLAMES SMELLED SO GOOD.
THE PATOLA MOUNTAIN RANGE-- WE'RE ALMOST THERE!
AANG, BEFORE WE GET TO THE TEMPLE, I WANT TO TALK TO YOU ABOUT THE AIRBENDERS.
WHAT ABOUT THEM?
WELL...I JUST WANT YOU TO BE PREPARED FOR WHAT YOU MIGHT SEE. THE FIRE NATION IS RUTHLESS.
THEY KILLED MY MOTHER. THEY COULD HAVE DONE THE SAME TO YOUR PEOPLE.
JUST BECAUSE NO ONE HAS SEEN AN AIRBENDER DOESN'T MEAN THAT THE FIRE NATION KILLED THEM ALL. THEY PROBABLY ESCAPED.

I KNOW IT'S HARD TO ACCEPT.
YOU DON'T UNDERSTAND. KATARA, THE ONLY WAY TO GET TO AN AIRBENDER TEMPLE IS ON A FLYING BISON. AND I DOUBT THE FIRE NATION HAS ANY FLYING BISON.
RIGHT, APPA?
YIP-YIP!
HRRMM
THERE IT IS...THE SOUTHERN AIR TEMPLE.
AANG, IT'S AMAZING!
WE'RE HOME, BUDDY. WE'RE HOME.

COMMANDER ZHAO'S TENT
AND BY YEAR'S END, THE EARTH KINGDOM CAPITAL WILL BE UNDER OUR RULE. THE FIRE LORD WILL FINALLY CLAIM VICTORY IN THIS WAR.
IF MY FATHER THINKS THE REST OF THE WORLD WILL FOLLOW HIM WILLINGLY, THEN HE IS A FOOL.
TWO YEARS AT SEA HAVE DONE LITTLE TO TEMPER YOUR TONGUE. SO...HOW IS YOUR SEARCH FOR THE AVATAR GOING?
CRASH
MY FAULT ENTIRELY.

WE HAVEN'T FOUND HIM YET.
DID YOU REALLY EXPECT TO? THE AVATAR DIED A HUNDRED YEARS AGO...ALONG WITH THE REST OF THE AIRBENDERS.
UNLESS YOU'VE FOUND SOME EVIDENCE THAT THE AVATAR IS ALIVE?
NO. NOTHING.
PRINCE ZUKO, THE AVATAR IS THE ONLY ONE WHO CAN STOP THE FIRE NATION FROM WINNING THIS WAR.
IF YOU HAVE AN OUNCE OF LOYALTY LEFT, YOU'LL TELL ME WHAT YOU FOUND.

I HAVEN'T FOUND ANYTHING. IT'S LIKE YOU SAID, THE AVATAR PROBABLY DIED A LONG TIME AGO.
COME ON, UNCLE. WE'RE GOING.
!
SHING
COMMANDER ZHAO, WE INTERROGATED THE CREW AS YOU INSTRUCTED. THEY CONFIRMED PRINCE ZUKO HAD THE AVATAR IN CUSTODY BUT LET HIM ESCAPE.
NOW REMIND ME-- HOW EXACTLY WAS YOUR SHIP DAMAGED?

SO WHERE DO I GET SOMETHING TO EAT?
YOU'RE LUCKY ENOUGH TO BE ONE OF THE FIRST OUTSIDERS TO EVER VISIT AN AIRBENDER TEMPLE, AND ALL YOU CAN THINK ABOUT IS FOOD?
I'M JUST A SIMPLE GUY WITH SIMPLE NEEDS.
SO THAT'S WHERE MY FRIENDS AND I WOULD PLAY AIRBALL...AND OVER THERE IS WHERE THE BISON WOULD SLEEP... AND-- ≑SIGH≑
WHAT'S WRONG?
THIS PLACE USED TO BE FULL OF MONKS AND LEMURS AND BISON. NOW THERE'S JUST A BUNCH OF WEEDS...
I CAN'T BELIEVE HOW MUCH THINGS HAVE CHANGED.
SO...UH, THIS AIRBALL GAME. HOW DO YOU PLAY?

THWUMP

AANG, SEVEN. SOKKA, ZERO.
MAKING HIM FEEL BETTER IS PUTTING ME IN A WORLD OF HURT.
KATARA, CHECK THIS OUT.
FIRE NATION.
WE SHOULD TELL HIM.

AANG, THERE'S SOMETHING YOU NEED TO SEE.
OKAY. WHAT IS IT?
SHWUMP
UH...JUST A NEW WATERBENDING MOVE I LEARNED.
NICE ONE. BUT ENOUGH PRACTICING. WE HAVE A WHOLE TEMPLE TO SEE!
YOU KNOW YOU CAN'T PROTECT HIM FOREVER.

KATARA, FIREBENDERS WERE HERE. YOU CAN'T PRETEND THEY WEREN'T.
I CAN FOR AANG'S SAKE. IF HE FINDS OUT THAT THE FIRE NATION INVADED HIS HOME, HE'LL BE DEVASTATED.
HEY, GUYS, I WANT YOU TO MEET SOMEBODY!
WHO'S THAT?
MONK GYATSO-- THE GREATEST AIRBENDER IN THE WORLD.
HE TAUGHT ME EVERYTHING I KNOW.

BUT THE TRUE SECRET...
...IS IN THE GOOEY CENTER.
HMMM.
MY ANCIENT CAKE MAKING TECHNIQUE ISN'T THE ONLY THING ON YOUR MIND, IS IT, AANG?
THIS WHOLE AVATAR THING... MAYBE THE MONKS MADE A MISTAKE?
THE ONLY MISTAKE THEY MADE WAS TELLING YOU BEFORE YOU TURNED SIXTEEN. BUT WE CAN'T CONCERN OURSELVES WITH WHAT WAS-- WE MUST ACT ON WHAT IS.
BUT, GYATSO, HOW DO I KNOW IF I'M READY FOR THIS?
YOUR QUESTIONS WILL BE ANSWERED WHEN YOU'RE OLD ENOUGH TO ENTER THE AIR TEMPLE SANCTUARY. INSIDE, YOU WILL MEET SOMEONE WHO WILL GUIDE YOU ON YOUR JOURNEY.

WHO IS IT?
WHEN YOU ARE READY, HE WILL REVEAL HIMSELF TO YOU.
AWW!
NOW, ARE YOU GOING TO HELP ME WITH THESE CAKES OR NOT?
ALL RIGHT.
ONE... TWO... THREE!

SPLAT
CHIRP
CHIRP
CHIRP
HAHAHA!
YOUR AIM HAS IMPROVED GREATLY, MY YOUNG PUPIL.

YOU MUST MISS HIM.
YEAH.
WHERE ARE YOU GOING?
THE AIR TEMPLE SANCTUARY. THERE'S SOMEONE I'M READY TO MEET.
BUT, AANG, NO ONE COULD HAVE SURVIVED IN THERE FOR A HUNDRED YEARS.
IT'S NOT IMPOSSIBLE. I SURVIVED IN THE ICEBERG FOR THAT LONG.
GOOD POINT.

KATARA, WHOEVER'S IN THERE MIGHT HELP ME FIGURE OUT THIS AVATAR THING.
AND WHOEVER'S IN THERE MIGHT HAVE A MEDLEY OF DELICIOUS CURED MEATS!
WHAM
I DON'T SUPPOSE YOU HAVE A KEY?
THE KEY, SOKKA, IS AIRBENDING.

CREEEAK
HELLO? ANYONE HOME?

COMMANDER ZHAO'S TENT
SO A TWELVE-YEAR-OLD BOY BESTED YOU AND YOUR FIREBENDERS? YOU'RE MORE PATHETIC THAN I THOUGHT.
I UNDERESTIMATED HIM ONCE, BUT IT WILL NOT HAPPEN AGAIN.
NO, IT WILL NOT. BECAUSE YOU WON'T HAVE A SECOND CHANCE.
COMMANDER ZHAO, I'VE BEEN HUNTING THE AVATAR FOR TWO YEARS AND I--
AND YOU'VE FAILED. CAPTURING THE AVATAR IS TOO IMPORTANT TO LEAVE IN A TEENAGER'S HANDS. HE'S MINE NOW.
GRRR!
KEEP THEM HERE.
SMASH
MORE TEA, PLEASE.

AIRBENDER SANCTUARY
STATUES? THAT'S IT? WHERE'S THE MEAT?
WHO ARE ALL THESE PEOPLE?
I'M NOT SURE. BUT IT FEELS LIKE I KNOW THEM SOMEHOW.

LOOK, THAT ONE'S AN AIRBENDER.
AND THIS ONE'S A WATERBENDER.
THEY'RE LINED UP IN A PATTERN: AIR, WATER, EARTH, AND FIRE.
THAT'S THE AVATAR CYCLE.
OF COURSE! THEY'RE AVATARS! ALL THESE PEOPLE ARE YOUR PAST LIVES, AANG.
WOW. THERE'S SO MANY.
PAST LIVES? KATARA, YOU REALLY BELIEVE IN THAT STUFF?
IT'S TRUE. WHEN THE AVATAR DIES, HE'S REINCARNATED INTO THE NEXT NATION IN THE CYCLE.

AANG, SNAP OUT OF IT.
HUH?
WHO IS THAT?
THAT'S AVATAR ROKU. THE AVATAR BEFORE ME.
YOU WERE A FIREBENDER? NO WONDER I DIDN'T TRUST YOU WHEN WE FIRST MET.
THERE'S NO WRITING. HOW DO YOU KNOW HIS NAME?

I'M NOT SURE. I JUST KNOW IT SOMEHOW.
YOU JUST COULDN'T GET ANY WEIRDER.
FFWSSSHHH
FIREBENDER. NOBODY MAKE A SOUND!
YOU'RE MAKING A SOUND--
SHHH!

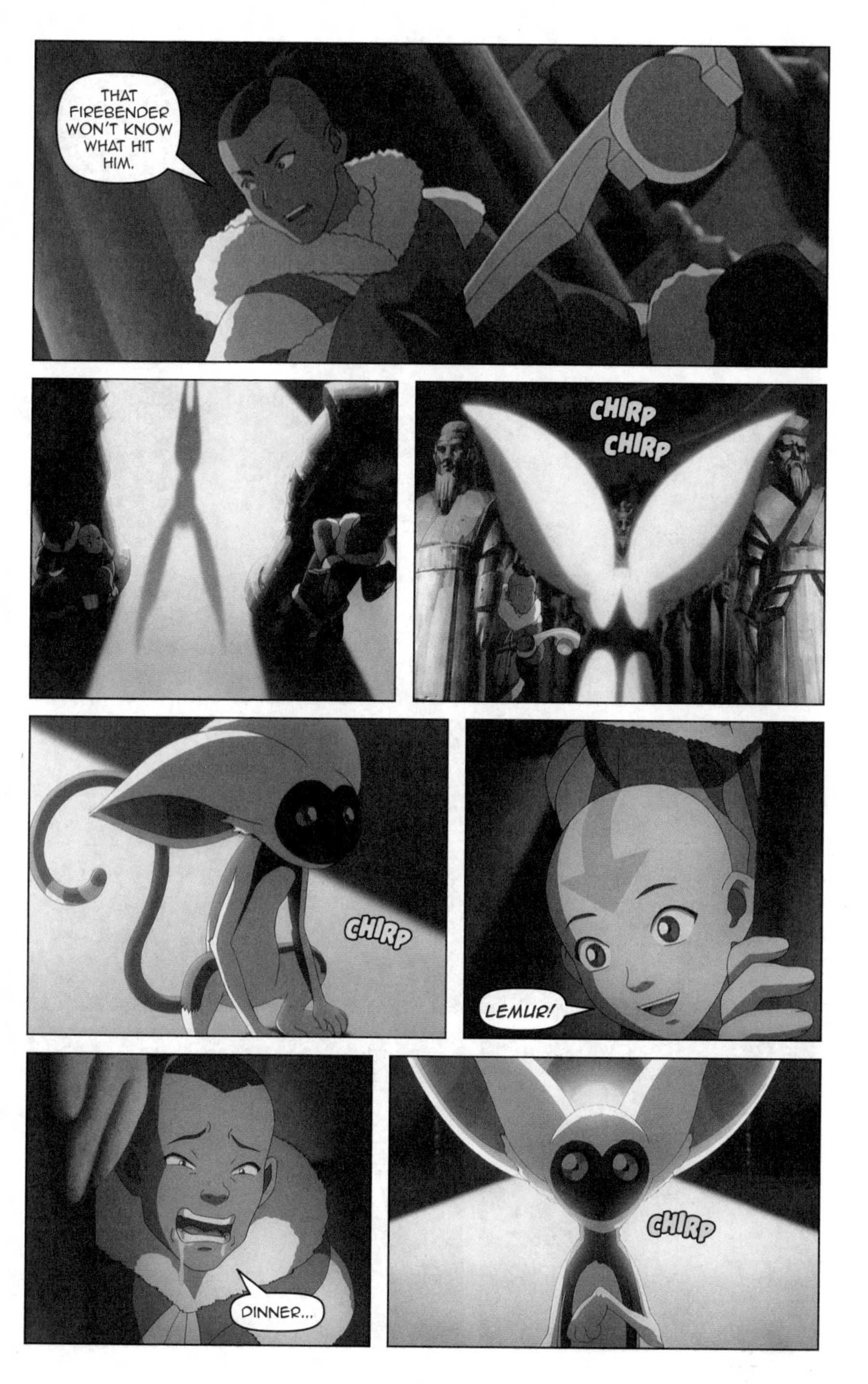
THAT FIREBENDER WON'T KNOW WHAT HIT HIM.
CHIRP
CHIRP
CHIRP
LEMUR!
DINNER...
CHIRP

DON'T LISTEN TO HIM. YOU'RE GOING TO BE MY NEW PET.
NOT IF I GET HIM FIRST.
WAIT, COME BACK.
I WANT TO EAT YOU!
OOF

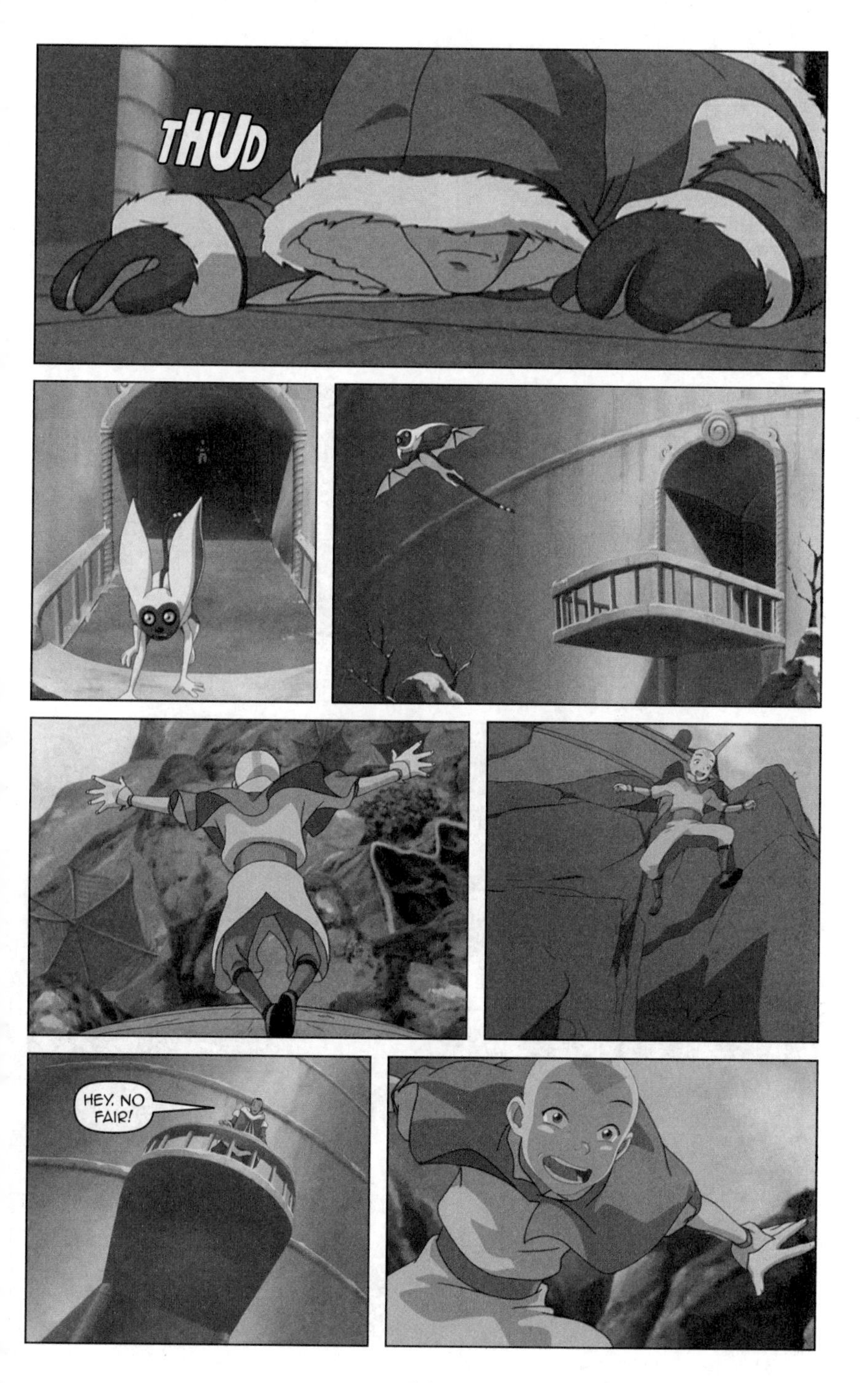
THUD
HEY, NO FAIR!

COMMANDER ZHAO'S TENT
MY SEARCH PARTY IS READY. ONCE I'M OUT TO SEA, MY GUARDS WILL ESCORT YOU BACK TO YOUR SHIP AND YOU WILL BE FREE TO GO.
WHY? ARE YOU WORRIED I'M GOING TO TRY AND STOP YOU?
YOU, STOP ME? IMPOSSIBLE.
DON'T UNDERESTIMATE ME, ZHAO. I *WILL* CAPTURE THE AVATAR BEFORE YOU.
PRINCE ZUKO, THAT'S ENOUGH.
YOU CAN'T COMPETE WITH ME. I HAVE HUNDREDS OF WARSHIPS UNDER MY COMMAND, AND YOU...YOU'RE JUST A BANISHED PRINCE.
NO HOME. NO ALLIES. YOUR OWN FATHER DOESN'T EVEN WANT YOU.
YOU'RE WRONG. ONCE I DELIVER THE AVATAR TO MY FATHER, HE WILL WELCOME ME HOME WITH HONOR--AND RESTORE MY RIGHTFUL PLACE ON THE THRONE.

IF YOUR FATHER REALLY WANTED YOU HOME, HE WOULD HAVE LET YOU RETURN BY NOW--AVATAR OR NO AVATAR. BUT IN HIS EYES, YOU ARE A FAILURE AND A DISGRACE TO THE FIRE NATION.
THAT'S NOT TRUE.
YOU HAVE THE SCAR TO PROVE IT.
MAYBE YOU'D LIKE ONE TO MATCH.
IS THAT A CHALLENGE?
AN AGNI KAI. AT SUNSET.
VERY WELL.
IT'S A SHAME YOUR FATHER WON'T BE HERE TO WATCH ME HUMILIATE YOU. I GUESS YOUR UNCLE WILL DO.
PRINCE ZUKO, HAVE YOU FORGOTTEN WHAT HAPPENED LAST TIME YOU DUELED A MASTER?
I WILL NEVER FORGET.

AIR TEMPLE
HEY, COME BACK!
COME ON OUT, LITTLE LEMUR. THAT HUNGRY GUY WON'T BOTHER YOU ANYMORE--

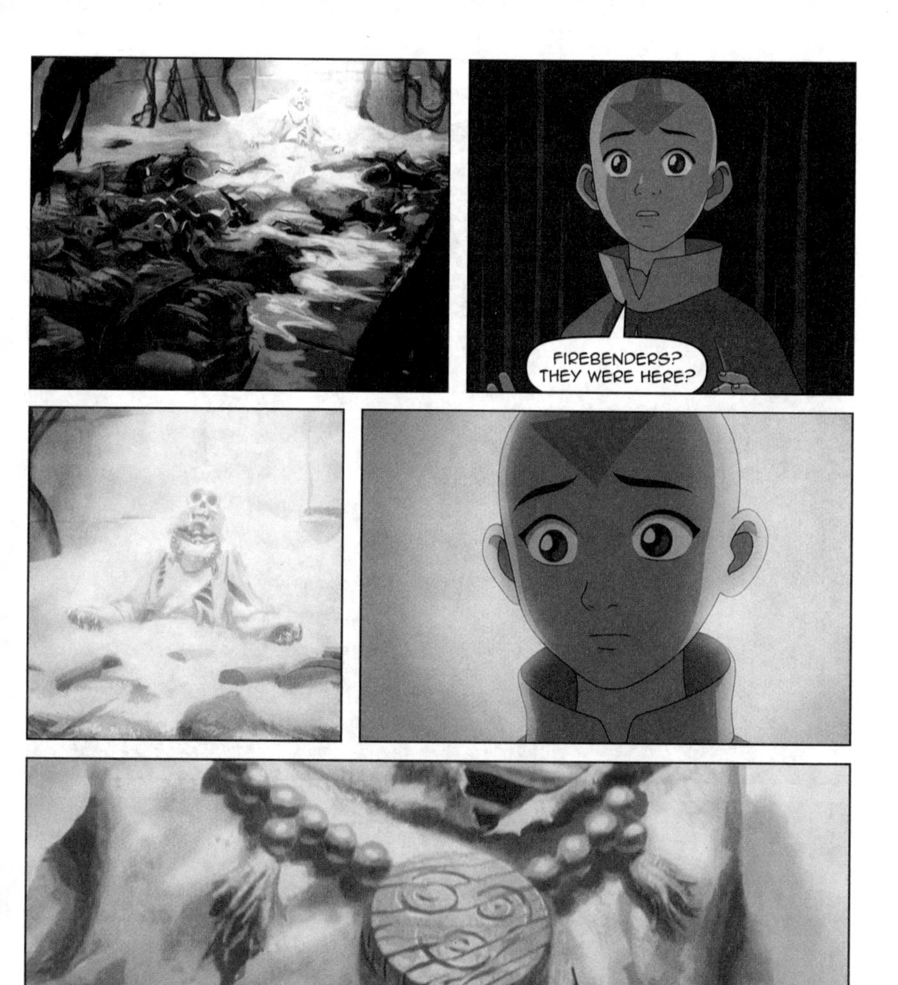
FIREBENDERS?
THEY WERE HERE?

GYATSO?
HEY, AANG, YOU FIND MY DINNER YET?

AANG, I WASN'T REALLY GONNA EAT THE LEMUR, OKAY?

OH, MAN.

COME ON, AANG, EVERYTHING WILL BE ALL RIGHT. LET'S GET OUT OF HERE.

GASP

AANG--

EARTH KINGDOM SANCTUARY
!
WATER TRIBE SANCTUARY
FIRE NATION SANCTUARY
SEND WORD TO THE FIRE LORD IMMEDIATELY. THE AVATAR HAS RETURNED.

AIR TEMPLE
AANG, COME ON, SNAP OUT OF IT!
KASHOOM

WHAT HAPPENED?
HE FOUND OUT FIREBENDERS KILLED GYATSO--
OH, NO! IT'S HIS AVATAR SPIRIT--HE MUST HAVE TRIGGERED IT!
I'M GONNA TRY AND CALM HIM DOWN!
WELL, DO IT BEFORE HE BLOWS US OFF THE MOUNTAIN!

LOADING DOCKS
REMEMBER YOUR FIREBENDING BASICS, PRINCE ZUKO. THEY ARE YOUR GREATEST WEAPON.
I REFUSE TO LET HIM WIN.
THIS WILL BE OVER QUICKLY.

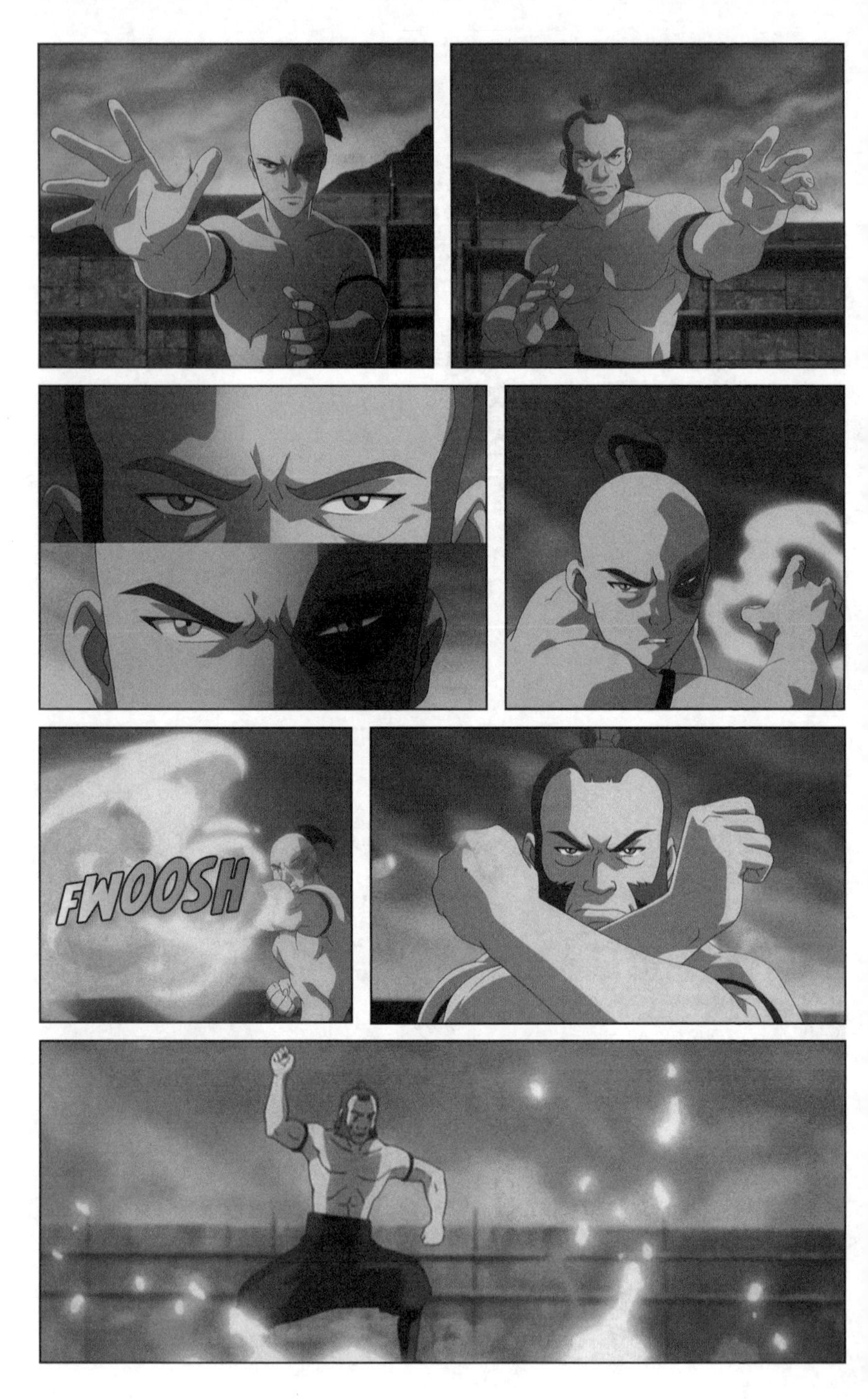
FWOOSH

BASICS, ZUKO. BREAK HIS ROOT!

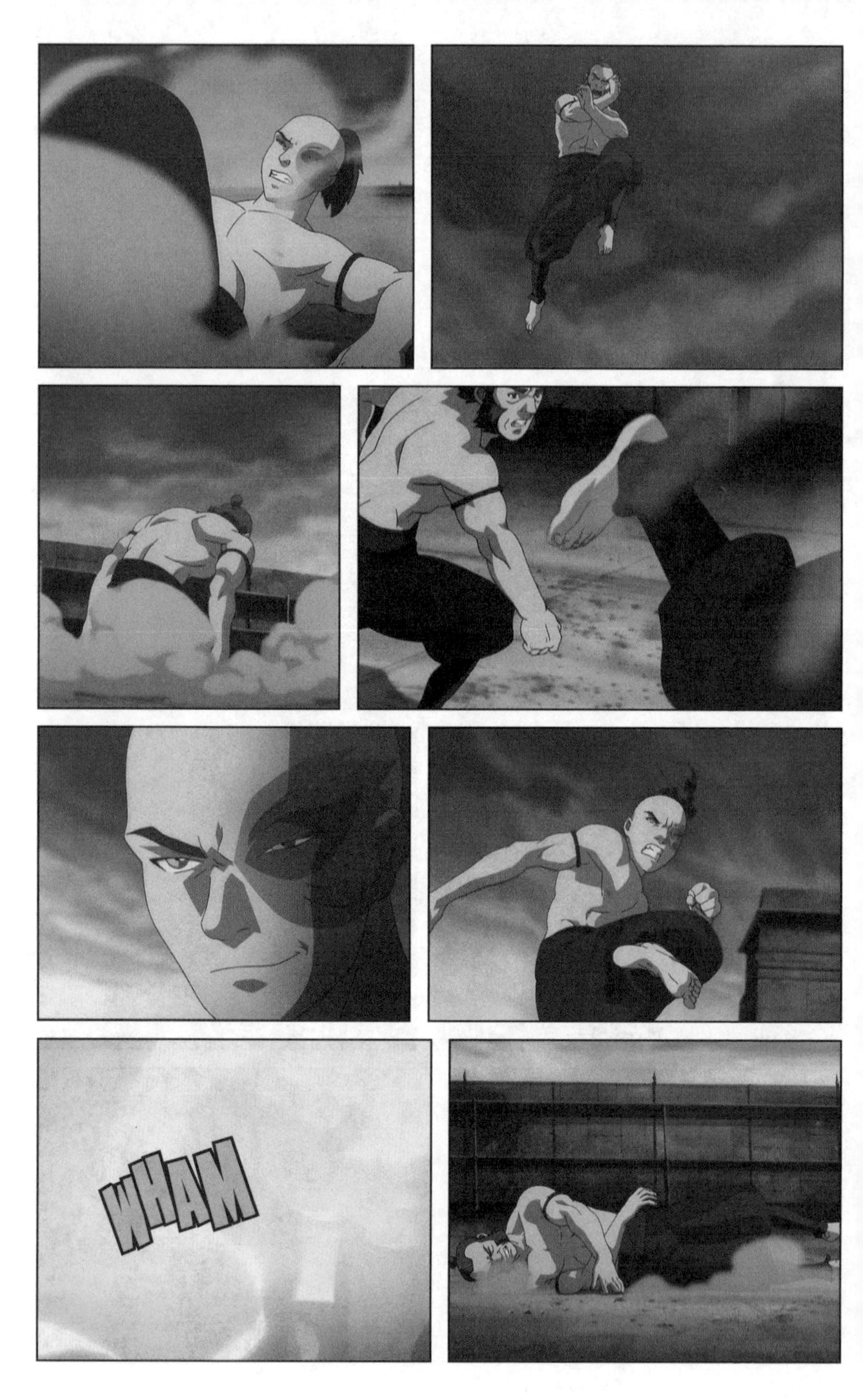
WHAM

DO IT.
FWOOSH
THAT'S IT? YOUR FATHER RAISED A COWARD.
NEXT TIME YOU GET IN MY WAY, I PROMISE... I WON'T HOLD BACK.

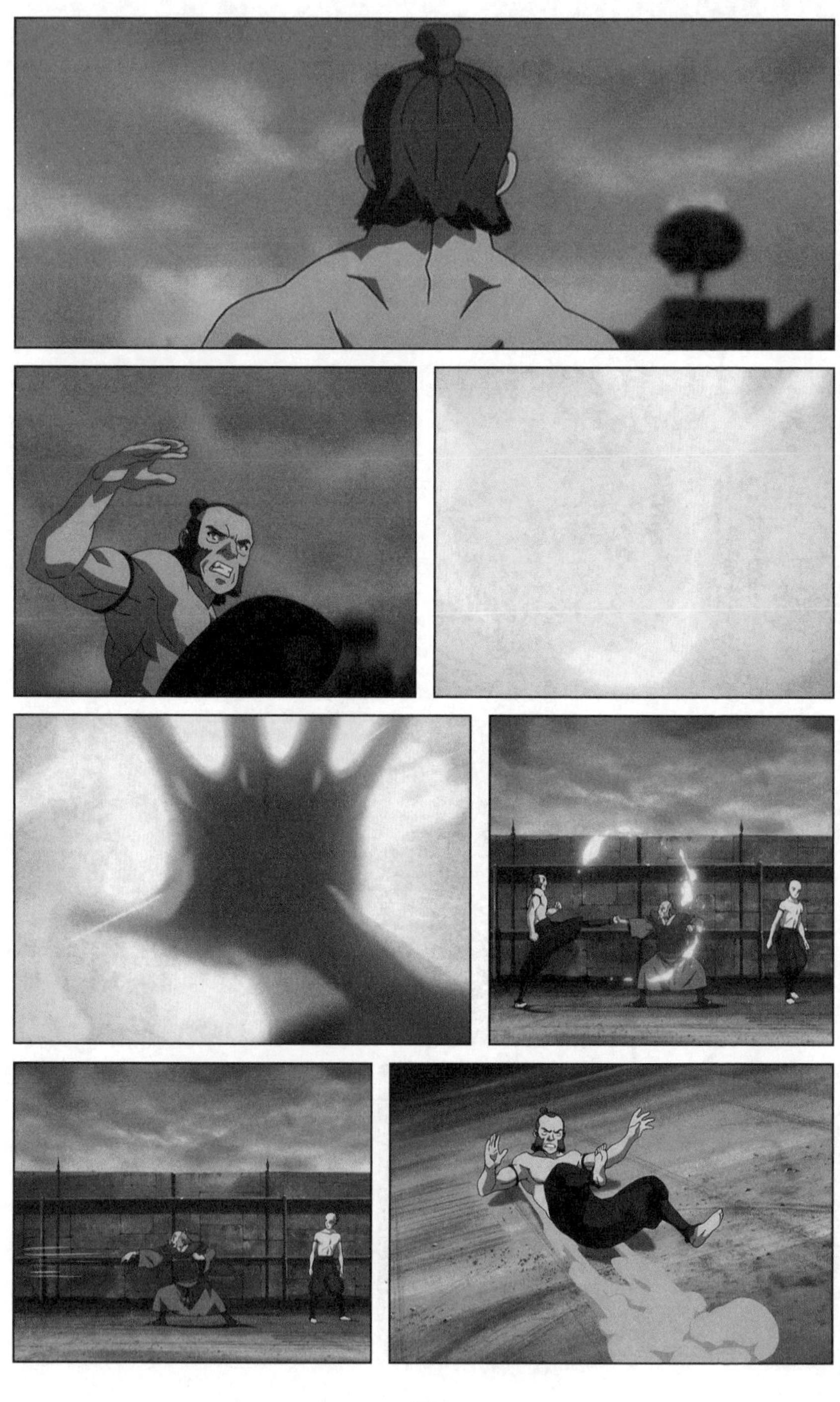

NO, PRINCE ZUKO. DO NOT TAINT YOUR VICTORY.
SO THIS IS HOW THE GREAT COMMANDER ZHAO ACTS IN DEFEAT? DISGRACEFUL. EVEN IN EXILE, MY NEPHEW IS MORE HONORABLE THAN YOU.
THANKS AGAIN FOR THE TEA. IT WAS DELICIOUS.
DID YOU REALLY MEAN THAT, UNCLE?
OF COURSE... I TOLD YOU GINSENG TEA IS MY FAVORITE.

AIR TEMPLE

AANG, I KNOW YOU'RE UPSET. AND I KNOW HOW HARD IT IS TO LOSE THE PEOPLE YOU LOVE. I WENT THROUGH THE SAME THING WHEN I LOST MY MOM.

MONK GYATSO AND THE OTHER AIRBENDERS MAY BE GONE, BUT YOU STILL HAVE A FAMILY. SOKKA AND I, WE'RE YOUR FAMILY NOW.

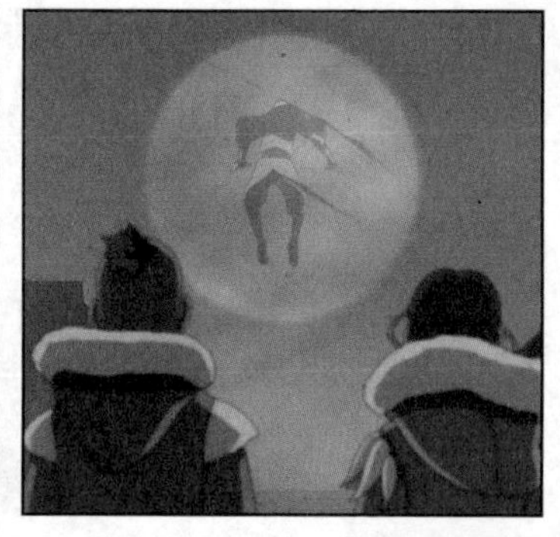

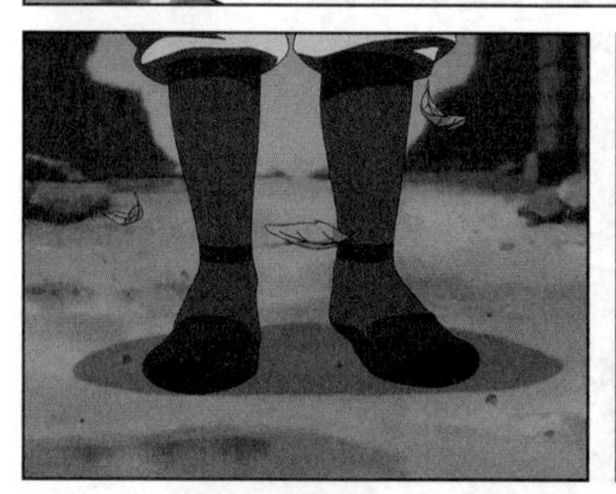

KATARA AND I AREN'T GOING TO LET ANYTHING HAPPEN TO YOU. PROMISE.

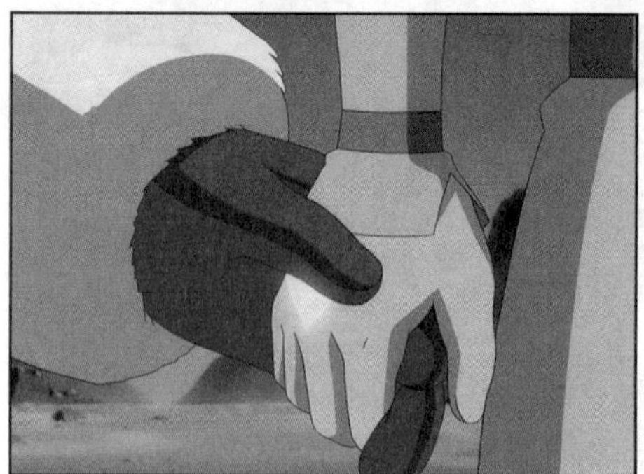

I'M SORRY.

IT'S OKAY. IT WASN'T YOUR FAULT.
BUT YOU WERE RIGHT. AND IF FIREBENDERS FOUND THIS TEMPLE, THAT MEANS THEY FOUND THE OTHER ONES, TOO.
I REALLY AM THE LAST AIRBENDER.
EVERYTHING'S PACKED. YOU READY TO GO?
HOW IS ROKU SUPPOSED TO HELP ME IF I CAN'T TALK TO HIM?
MAYBE YOU'LL FIND A WAY.

CHIRP
CAN'T TALK. MUST EAT.
LOOKS LIKE YOU MADE A NEW FRIEND, SOKKA.
MRRRRP
HEY, LITTLE GUY.

YOU, ME, AND APPA. WE'RE ALL THAT'S LEFT OF THIS PLACE. WE HAVE TO STICK TOGETHER.
KATARA, SOKKA, SAY HELLO TO THE NEWEST MEMBER OF OUR FAMILY.
WHAT ARE YOU GOING TO NAME HIM?
MOMO.
HAHAHA

CHAPTER FOUR

THE WARRIORS OF KYOSHI

ZUKO'S QUARTERS
THE ONLY REASON YOU SHOULD BE INTERRUPTING ME IS IF YOU HAVE NEWS ABOUT THE AVATAR.
WELL, THERE IS NEWS, PRINCE ZUKO, BUT YOU MIGHT NOT LIKE IT. DON'T GET TOO UPSET...
UNCLE, YOU TAUGHT ME THAT KEEPING A LEVEL HEAD IS A SIGN OF A GREAT LEADER.
NOW, WHATEVER YOU HAVE TO SAY, I'M SURE I CAN TAKE IT.

OKAY THEN. WE HAVE NO IDEA WHERE HE IS.
WHAT?!
YOU REALLY SHOULD OPEN A WINDOW IN HERE.
GIVE ME THE MAP!
THERE HAVE BEEN MULTIPLE SIGHTINGS OF THE AVATAR, BUT HE'S IMPOSSIBLE TO TRACK DOWN.
HOW AM I GOING TO FIND HIM, UNCLE? HE IS CLEARLY A MASTER OF EVASIVE MANEUVERING.
THE SOUTH SEA
YOU HAVE NO IDEA WHERE YOU'RE GOING, DO YOU?
WELL, I KNOW IT'S NEAR WATER...

I GUESS WE'RE GETTING CLOSE, THEN.
MOMO, MARBLES, PLEASE.
HEY, KATARA, CHECK OUT THIS AIRBENDING TRICK.
THAT'S GREAT, AANG.
YOU DIDN'T EVEN LOOK.
THAT'S GREAT!
BUT I'M NOT DOING IT NOW.
STOP BUGGING HER, AIRHEAD. YOU NEED TO GIVE GIRLS SPACE WHEN THEY DO THEIR SEWING.

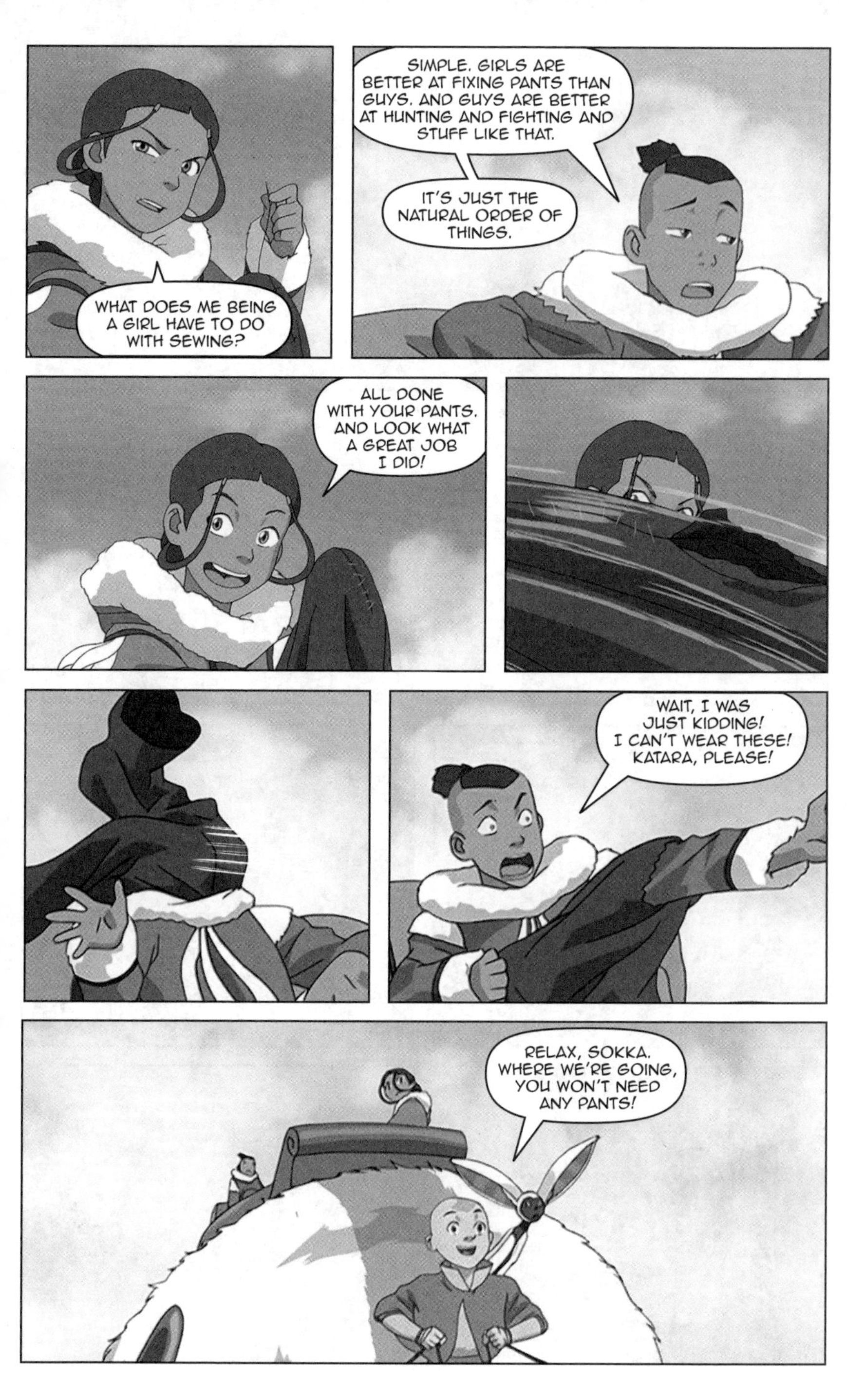
WHAT DOES ME BEING A GIRL HAVE TO DO WITH SEWING?
SIMPLE. GIRLS ARE BETTER AT FIXING PANTS THAN GUYS. AND GUYS ARE BETTER AT HUNTING AND FIGHTING AND STUFF LIKE THAT.
IT'S JUST THE NATURAL ORDER OF THINGS.
ALL DONE WITH YOUR PANTS. AND LOOK WHAT A GREAT JOB I DID!
WAIT, I WAS JUST KIDDING! I CAN'T WEAR THESE! KATARA, PLEASE!
RELAX, SOKKA. WHERE WE'RE GOING, YOU WON'T NEED ANY PANTS!

KYOSHI ISLAND
WE JUST MADE A PIT STOP YESTERDAY. SHOULDN'T WE GET A LITTLE MORE FLYING DONE BEFORE WE CAMP OUT?
HE'S RIGHT. AT THIS RATE, WE WON'T GET TO THE NORTH POLE UNTIL SPRING.
BUT APPA'S TIRED ALREADY, AREN'T YOU, BOY?
HRRRMM
YEAH, THAT WAS REAL CONVINCING. STILL, HARD TO ARGUE WITH A TEN-TON MAGICAL MONSTER.
I SAID, AREN'T YOU, BOY?
LOOK!

THAT'S WHY WE'RE HERE. ELEPHANT KOI. AND I'M GONNA RIDE THEM. KATARA, YOU GOTTA WATCH ME!
COLD!

YEAHHHHHH
HE LOOKS PRETTY GOOD OUT THERE.
ARE YOU KIDDING? THE FISH IS DOING ALL THE WORK.
NO, APPA! DON'T EAT THAT!
AW, MAN...

THERE'S SOMETHING IN THE WATER!
AANG'S IN TROUBLE! AANG!
GET OUT OF THERE!
COME IN!
GET BACK HERE, AANG!
WHOA
SPLASH
AHH!

WHAM
WHAT WAS THAT THING?
I DON'T KNOW.
WELL, LET'S NOT STICK AROUND TO FIND OUT. TIME TO HIT THE ROAD.
HUH?
AHH!
UGH!
OR WE COULD STAY A WHILE.

YOU THREE HAVE SOME EXPLAINING TO DO.
SHOW YOURSELVES, COWARDS!
AND IF YOU DON'T ANSWER ALL OUR QUESTIONS, WE'RE THROWING YOU BACK IN THE WATER WITH THE UNAGI.
WHO ARE YOU? WHERE ARE THE MEN WHO AMBUSHED US?
THERE WERE NO MEN-- WE AMBUSHED YOU. NOW TELL US, WHO ARE YOU AND WHAT ARE YOU DOING HERE?
WAIT A SECOND-- THERE'S NO WAY A BUNCH OF GIRLS TOOK US DOWN!
A BUNCH OF GIRLS, HUH? THE UNAGI'S GONNA EAT WELL TONIGHT.

NO, DON'T HURT HIM. HE DIDN'T MEAN IT. MY BROTHER'S JUST AN IDIOT SOMETIMES.
IT'S MY FAULT. I'M SORRY WE CAME HERE. I WANTED TO RIDE THE ELEPHANT KOI.
HOW DO WE KNOW YOU'RE NOT FIRE NATION SPIES? KYOSHI'S STAYED OUT OF THE WAR SO FAR, AND WE INTEND TO KEEP IT THAT WAY.
THIS ISLAND IS NAMED FOR KYOSHI? I KNOW KYOSHI!
HA! HOW COULD YOU POSSIBLY KNOW HER? AVATAR KYOSHI WAS BORN HERE FOUR HUNDRED YEARS AGO.
SHE'S BEEN DEAD FOR CENTURIES.
I KNOW HER BECAUSE I'M THE AVATAR.

THAT'S IMPOSSIBLE. THE LAST AVATAR WAS AN AIRBENDER WHO DISAPPEARED A HUNDRED YEARS AGO.
THAT'S ME.
THROW THE IMPOSTOR TO THE UNAGI.
AANG, DO SOME AIRBENDING!

NOW CHECK THIS OUT.
IT'S TRUE... YOU ARE THE AVATAR!
YAY!
YAY!

DID YOU HEAR THE NEWS? THE AVATAR'S ON KYOSHI!
!
!
THE AVATAR'S ON KYOSHI ISLAND?
UNCLE, READY THE RHINOS. HE'S NOT GETTING AWAY FROM ME THIS TIME.
ARE YOU GOING TO FINISH THAT?
I WAS GOING TO SAVE IT FOR LATER!

ALL RIGHT! DESSERT FOR BREAKFAST! THESE PEOPLE SURE KNOW HOW TO TREAT AN AVATAR.
MMM. KATARA, YOU GOTTA TRY THESE.
WELL, MAYBE JUST A BITE.
SOKKA, WHAT'S YOUR PROBLEM? EAT!
NOT HUNGRY.
BUT YOU'RE ALWAYS HUNGRY.

THEY SNUCK UP ON ME.
HE'S JUST UPSET BECAUSE A BUNCH OF GIRLS KICKED HIS BUTT YESTERDAY.
RIGHT. AND THEN THEY KICKED YOUR BUTT.
SNEAK ATTACKS DON'T COUNT.
TIE ME UP WITH ROPES... I'LL SHOW THEM A THING OR TWO...
I'M NOT SCARED OF ANY GIRLS... WHO DO THEY THINK THEY ARE ANYWAY?
MMM, THIS IS TASTY.
WHAT'S HE SO ANGRY ABOUT? IT'S GREAT HERE. THEY'RE GIVING US THE ROYAL TREATMENT.

HEY, DON'T GET TOO COMFORTABLE. IT'S RISKY FOR US TO STAY IN ONE PLACE FOR VERY LONG.
I'M SURE WE'LL BE FINE. BESIDES, DID YOU SEE HOW HAPPY I'M MAKING THIS TOWN? THEY'RE EVEN CLEANING OFF THAT STATUE IN MY HONOR.
WELL, IT'S NICE TO SEE YOU EXCITED ABOUT BEING THE AVATAR. I JUST HOPE IT DOESN'T ALL GO TO YOUR HEAD.
COME ON, YOU KNOW ME BETTER THAN THAT. I'M JUST A SIMPLE MONK.

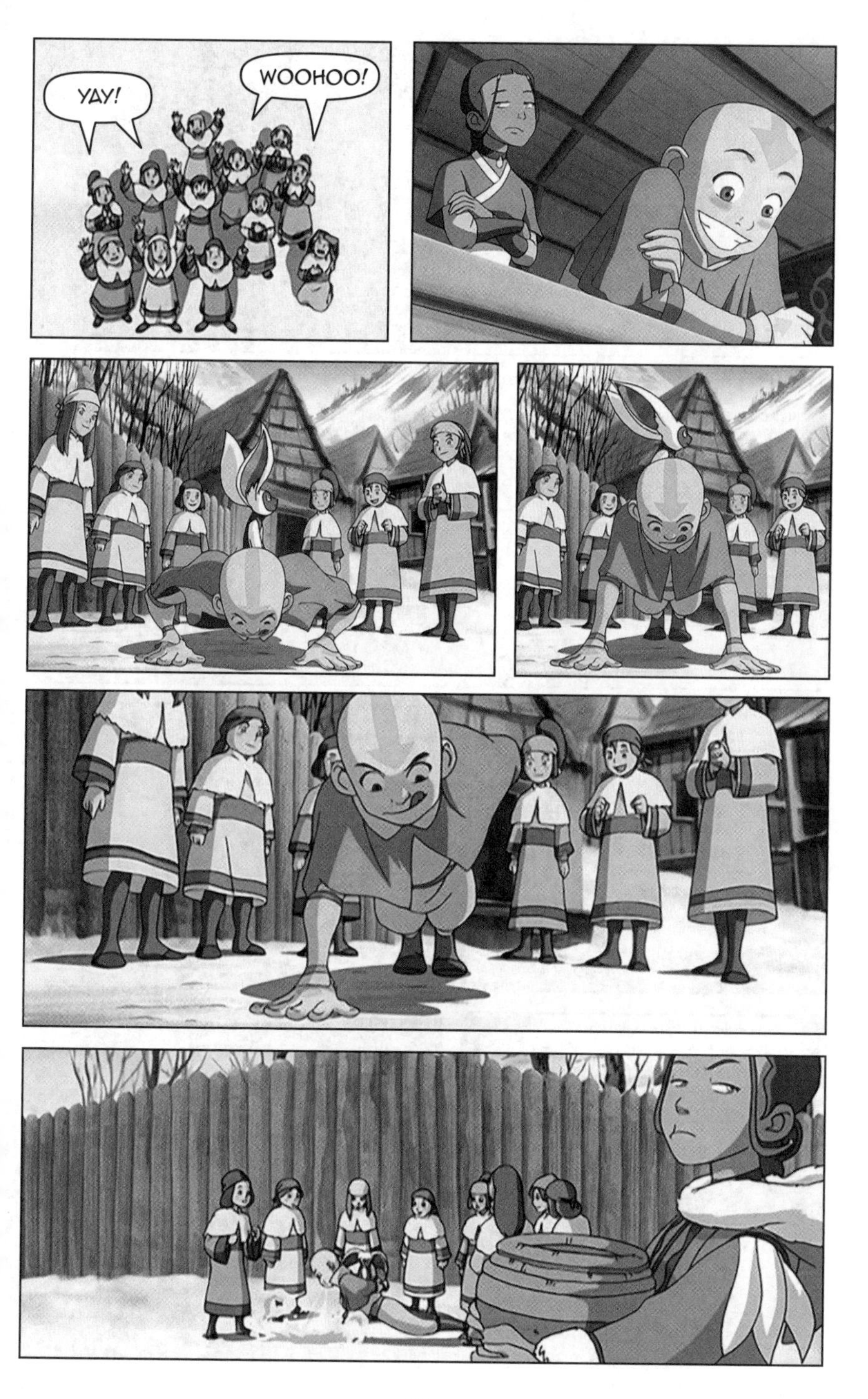
YAY!
WOOHOO!

I CAN'T BELIEVE IT. I GOT BEAT UP BY A BUNCH OF GIRLS.
SORRY, LADIES, DIDN'T MEAN TO INTERRUPT YOUR DANCE LESSON. I WAS JUST LOOKING FOR SOMEWHERE TO GET A LITTLE WORKOUT.
WELL, YOU'RE IN THE RIGHT PLACE. SORRY ABOUT YESTERDAY. I DIDN'T KNOW YOU WERE FRIENDS WITH THE AVATAR...
IT'S ALL RIGHT. I MEAN, NORMALLY I'D HOLD A GRUDGE...
BUT SEEING AS YOU GUYS ARE A BUNCH OF GIRLS, I'LL MAKE AN EXCEPTION.
I SHOULD HOPE SO. A BIG STRONG MAN LIKE YOU? WE WOULDN'T STAND A CHANCE.

TRUE. BUT DON'T FEEL BAD. AFTER ALL, I'M THE BEST WARRIOR IN MY VILLAGE.
WOW, BEST WARRIOR, HUH? IN YOUR WHOLE VILLAGE? MAYBE YOU'D BE KIND ENOUGH TO GIVE US A LITTLE DEMONSTRATION.
OH, WELL, I MEAN, I...
COME ON, GIRLS, WOULDN'T YOU LIKE HIM TO SHOW US SOME MOVES?
WELL, IF THAT'S WHAT YOU WANT, I'D BE HAPPY TO.
ALL RIGHT, YOU STAND OVER THERE...
NOW, THIS MAY BE A LITTLE TOUGH, BUT TRY TO BLOCK ME.

THWHACK
GOOD. OF COURSE, I WAS GOING EASY ON YOU...
OF COURSE.
LET'S SEE IF YOU CAN HANDLE THIS...
OOOF!

THAT DOES IT!
ANYTHING ELSE YOU WANT TO TEACH US?
TEE HEE.

THERE SHE IS, GIRLS. ME IN A PAST LIFE.
YOU WERE PRETTY.
EXCUSE ME FOR A SECOND, LADIES.
OH, GOOD. CAN YOU HELP ME CARRY THIS BACK TO THE ROOM? IT'S A LITTLE HEAVY.
ACTUALLY, I CAN'T RIGHT NOW.
WHAT DO YOU MEAN, YOU CAN'T?
I PROMISED THE GIRLS I'D GIVE 'EM A RIDE ON APPA. WHY DON'T YOU COME WITH US? IT'LL BE FUN.
WATCHING YOU SHOW OFF FOR A BUNCH OF GIRLS DOES NOT SOUND LIKE FUN.

WELL, NEITHER DOES CARRYING YOUR BASKET.
IT'S NOT MY BASKET. THESE SUPPLIES ARE FOR OUR TRIP. I TOLD YOU WE HAVE TO LEAVE KYOSHI SOON.
I DON'T WANT TO LEAVE KYOSHI YET. I CAN'T PUT MY FINGER ON IT, BUT THERE'S SOMETHING I REALLY LIKE ABOUT THIS PLACE.
WHAT'S TAKING YOU SO LONG, AANGY?
AANGY?
JUST A SECOND, KOKO!
SIMPLE MONK, HUH? I THOUGHT YOU PROMISED ME THIS AVATAR STUFF WOULDN'T GO TO YOUR HEAD.
IT DIDN'T.
YOU KNOW WHAT I THINK? YOU JUST DON'T WANT TO COME BECAUSE YOU'RE JEALOUS.

JEALOUS?! OF WHAT?
JEALOUS THAT WE'RE HAVING SO MUCH FUN WITHOUT YOU.
THAT'S RIDICULOUS!
IT *IS* A LITTLE RIDICULOUS, BUT I UNDERSTAND.
UGH!

UH...HEY, SUKI.
HOPING FOR ANOTHER DANCE LESSON?
NO. I--WELL, LET ME EXPLAIN...
SPIT IT OUT! WHAT DO YOU WANT?
I WOULD BE HONORED IF YOU WOULD TEACH ME.
EVEN IF I'M A GIRL?
I'M SORRY IF I INSULTED YOU EARLIER. I WAS WRONG.
WE NORMALLY DON'T TEACH OUTSIDERS, LET ALONE BOYS.
PLEASE MAKE AN EXCEPTION. I WON'T LET YOU DOWN.

ALL RIGHT, BUT YOU HAVE TO FOLLOW ALL OF OUR TRADITIONS.
OF COURSE.
AND I MEAN ALL OF THEM.
SOON...
DO I REALLY HAVE TO WEAR THIS? IT FEELS A LITTLE...GIRLIE.
IT'S A WARRIOR'S UNIFORM. YOU SHOULD BE PROUD.
THE SILK THREAD SYMBOLIZES THE BRAVE BLOOD THAT FLOWS THROUGH OUR VEINS.
THE GOLD INSIGNIA REPRESENTS THE HONOR OF THE WARRIOR'S HEART.
BRAVERY AND HONOR.
HEY, SOKKA, NICE DRESS.

KATARA, REMEMBER HOW THE UNAGI ALMOST GOT ME YESTERDAY?
YEAH.
WELL, I'M GONNA GO RIDE IT NOW. IT'S GONNA BE REAL DANGEROUS.
GOOD FOR YOU.
YOU'RE NOT GOING TO STOP ME?
NOPE. HAVE FUN.
I WILL.
GREAT.
I KNOW IT'S GREAT.
I'M GLAD YOU KNOW.
I'M GLAD YOU'RE GLAD.
GOOD.
FINE.

YOU'RE NOT GOING TO MASTER IT IN ONE DAY. EVEN *I'M* NOT THAT GOOD.
I THINK I'M STARTING TO GET IT.
IT'S NOT ABOUT STRENGTH. OUR TECHNIQUE IS ABOUT USING YOUR OPPONENT'S FORCE AGAINST THEM.

LOOSEN UP. THINK OF THE FAN AS AN EXTENSION OF YOUR ARM. WAIT FOR AN OPENING, AND THEN--
I FELL ON PURPOSE TO MAKE YOU FEEL BETTER.
I GOT YOU. ADMIT I GOT YOU!
OKAY, IT WAS A LUCKY SHOT. LET'S SEE IF YOU CAN DO IT AGAIN.
AHHH!

WHAT'S TAKING SO LONG?
I'M SURE IT'LL BE HERE ANY SECOND.
UH, WHAT ABOUT THIS?
NOT THAT AGAIN. BORING.
WHERE'S THE UNAGI? IT'S GETTING LATE.
WHERE ARE YOU GOING? DON'T LEAVE.
SORRY, AANG. MAYBE NEXT TIME.

KATARA! YOU SHOWED UP.
I WANTED TO MAKE SURE YOU WERE SAFE. YOU REALLY HAD ME WORRIED.
BUT BACK THERE YOU ACTED LIKE YOU DIDN'T CARE.
I'M SORRY.
ME TOO. I DID LET ALL THAT ATTENTION GO TO MY HEAD. I WAS BEING A JERK.
WELL, GET OUT OF THE WATER BEFORE YOU CATCH A COLD, YOU BIG JERK.
ON MY WAY.

AHHHH!

FWOOSH
AAAUGGGHHH!
SNAP
AAAUGGGHHH!
AAAUGGGHHH!
HANG ON, AANG!
AHHHH!

AANG!
SPLOOSH

ZUKO!

WHUMP
SNARL
SNARL
I WANT THE AVATAR ALIVE.
WAKE UP, AANG!

=COUGH=
KATARA...
DON'T RIDE THE UNAGI. NOT FUN.

NOT BAD.
FIREBENDERS HAVE LANDED ON OUR SHORES. GIRLS, COME QUICKLY!
HEY, I'M NOT A--
WHATEVER.

COME ON OUT, AVATAR! YOU CAN'T HIDE FROM ME FOREVER!
FIND HIM.
WHAM

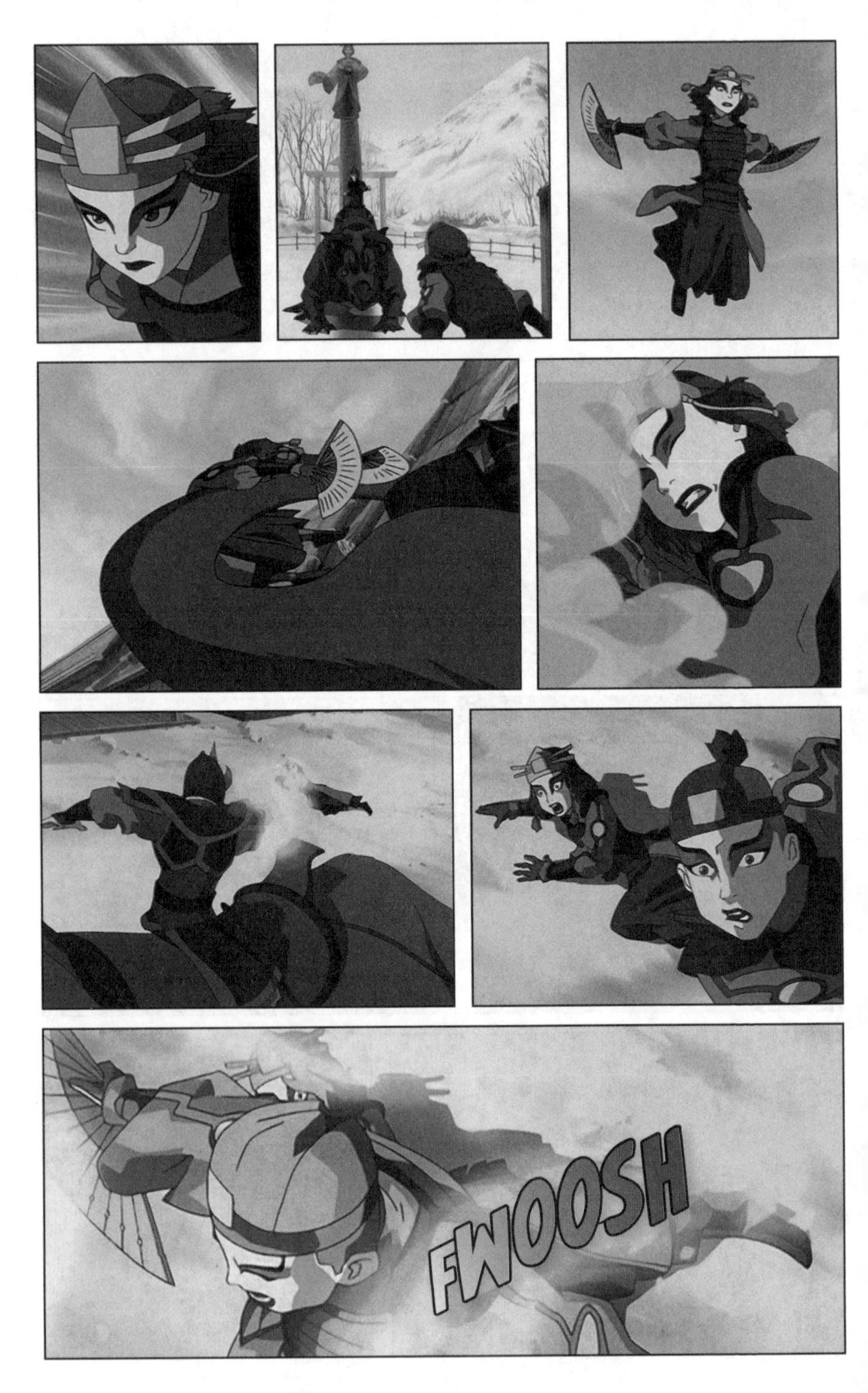
FWOOSH

WHUMP
I GUESS TRAINING'S OVER.
NICE TRY, AVATAR! BUT THESE LITTLE GIRLS CAN'T SAVE YOU!
HEY! OVER HERE!

FINALLY.
FWOOSH
CRASH

GET INSIDE.
LOOK WHAT I BROUGHT TO THIS PLACE.
IT'S NOT YOUR FAULT.
YES, IT IS. THESE PEOPLE GOT THEIR TOWN DESTROYED TRYING TO PROTECT ME.
THEN LET'S GET OUT OF HERE. ZUKO WILL LEAVE KYOSHI TO FOLLOW US.
I KNOW IT FEELS WRONG TO RUN, BUT I THINK IT'S THE ONLY WAY.
I'LL CALL APPA.

THERE'S NO TIME TO SAY GOODBYE.
WHAT ABOUT "I'M SORRY"?
FOR WHAT?
I TREATED YOU LIKE A GIRL WHEN I SHOULD HAVE TREATED YOU LIKE A WARRIOR.
I AM A WARRIOR...
BUT I'M A GIRL, TOO.

NOW GET OUT OF HERE. WE'LL HOLD THEM OFF.
APPA, YIP-YIP!
BACK TO THE SHIP! DON'T LOSE SIGHT OF THEM!
I KNOW IT'S HARD, BUT YOU DID THE RIGHT THING. ZUKO WOULD HAVE DESTROYED THE WHOLE PLACE IF WE STAYED.
THEY'RE GOING TO BE OKAY, AANG.
WHAT ARE YOU DOING?!

SPLASH

THANK YOU, AVATAR.
I KNOW, I KNOW. THAT WAS STUPID AND DANGEROUS.
YES. IT WAS.

CHAPTER FIVE

THE KING OF OMASHU

CITY OF OMASHU
THE EARTH KINGDOM CITY OF OMASHU.
I USED TO ALWAYS COME HERE TO VISIT MY FRIEND BUMI.
WOW. WE DON'T HAVE CITIES LIKE THIS IN THE SOUTH POLE.
THEY HAVE BUILDINGS HERE THAT DON'T MELT!
WELL, LET'S GO, SLOWPOKES! THE REAL FUN IS INSIDE THE CITY.
WAIT, AANG! IT COULD BE DANGEROUS IF PEOPLE FIND OUT YOU'RE THE AVATAR.
YOU NEED A DISGUISE.
SO...WHAT AM I SUPPOSED TO DO, GROW A MUSTACHE?

THIS IS SO ITCHY.
HOW DO YOU LIVE IN THIS STUFF?
GREAT. NOW YOU LOOK JUST LIKE MY GRANDFATHER.
TECHNICALLY, AANG IS 112 YEARS OLD.
NOW LET'S GET TO SKIPPIN', YOUNG WHIPPERSNAPPERS. THE BIG CITY AWAITS.

YOU GUYS ARE GONNA LOVE OMASHU. THE PEOPLE HERE ARE THE FRIENDLIEST IN THE WORLD.
ROTTEN CABBAGES! WHAT KIND OF SLUM DO YOU THINK THIS IS?!
CRACK
BOOM

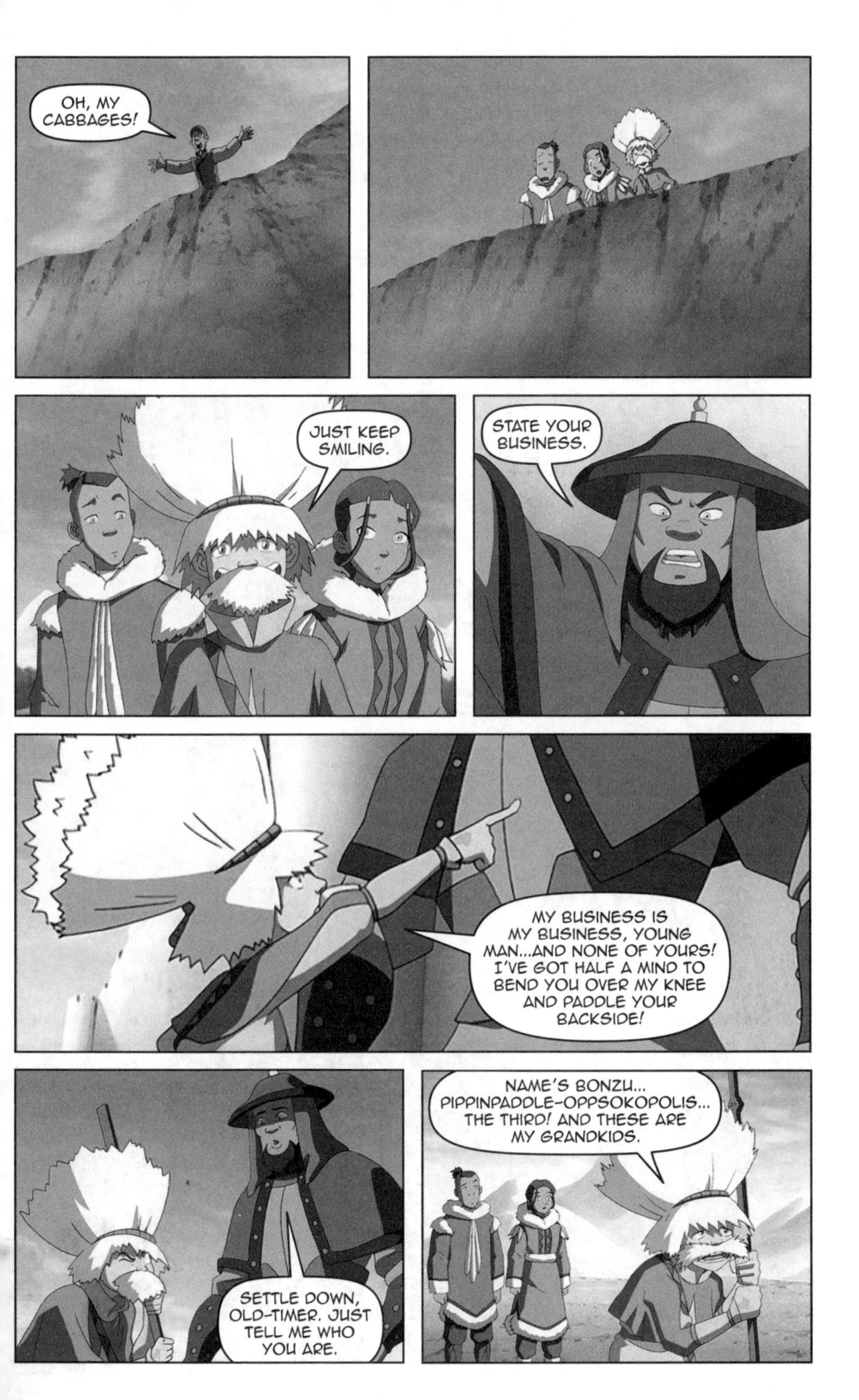
OH, MY CABBAGES!
JUST KEEP SMILING.
STATE YOUR BUSINESS.
MY BUSINESS IS MY BUSINESS, YOUNG MAN...AND NONE OF YOURS! I'VE GOT HALF A MIND TO BEND YOU OVER MY KNEE AND PADDLE YOUR BACKSIDE!
SETTLE DOWN, OLD-TIMER. JUST TELL ME WHO YOU ARE.
NAME'S BONZU... PIPPINPADDLE-OPPSOKOPOLIS... THE THIRD! AND THESE ARE MY GRANDKIDS.

HI, JUNE PIPPINPADDLE-OPPSOKOPOLIS, NICE TO MEET YOU.
YOU SEEM LIKE A RESPONSIBLE YOUNG LADY. SEE THAT YOUR GRANDFATHER STAYS OUT OF TROUBLE. ENJOY OMASHU.
WE WILL!
WAIT A MINUTE!
YOU'RE A STRONG YOUNG BOY. SHOW SOME RESPECT FOR THE ELDERLY AND CARRY YOUR GRANDFATHER'S BAG.
GOOD IDEA.
POINK

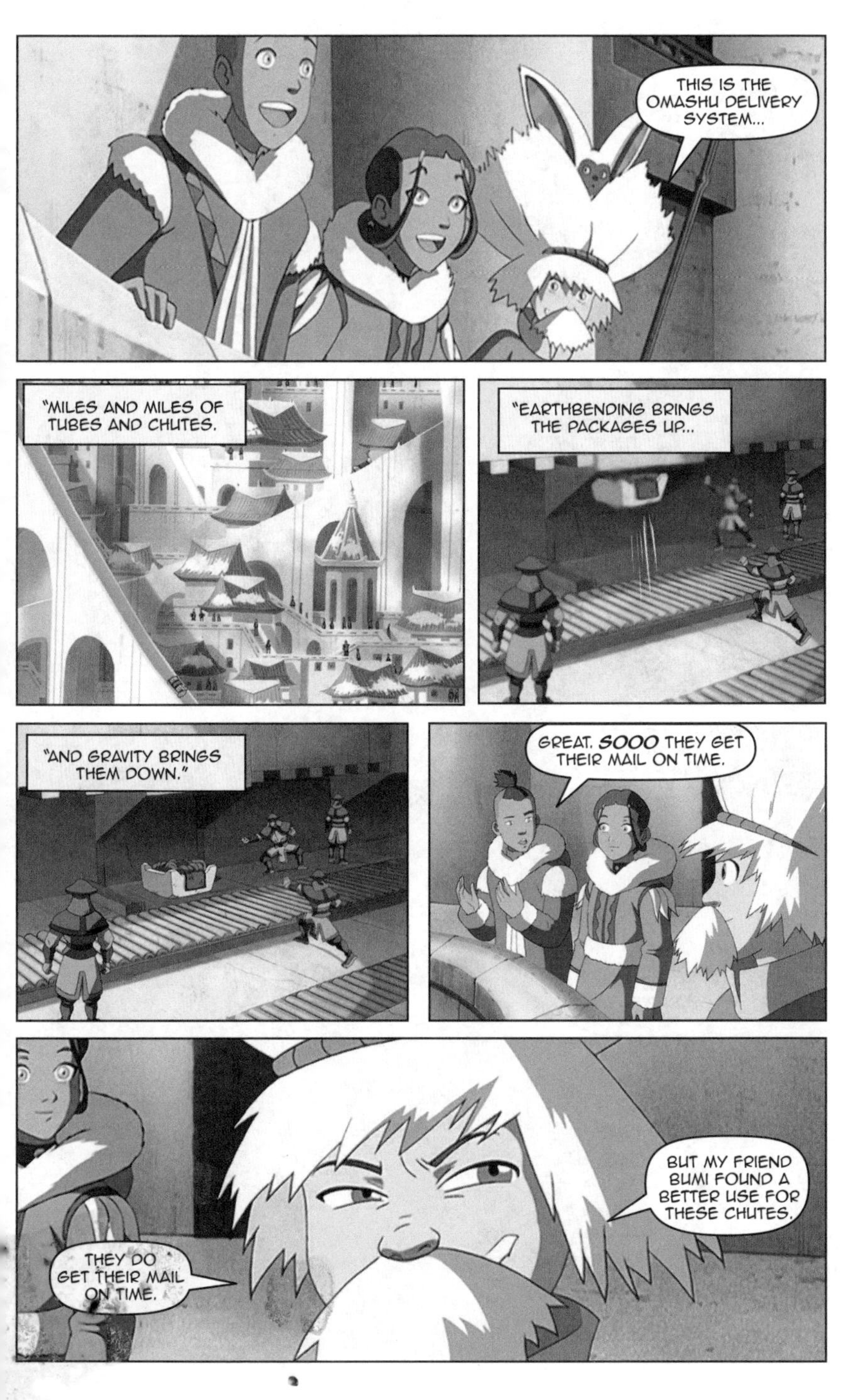
THIS IS THE OMASHU DELIVERY SYSTEM...
"MILES AND MILES OF TUBES AND CHUTES.
"EARTHBENDING BRINGS THE PACKAGES UP...
"AND GRAVITY BRINGS THEM DOWN."
GREAT. SOOO THEY GET THEIR MAIL ON TIME.
BUT MY FRIEND BUMI FOUND A BETTER USE FOR THESE CHUTES.
THEY DO GET THEIR MAIL ON TIME.

LOOK AROUND YOU. WHAT DO YOU SEE?
UM... THE MAIL SYSTEM?
INSTEAD OF SEEING WHAT THEY WANT YOU TO SEE, YOU GOTTA OPEN YOUR BRAIN TO THE POSSIBILITIES.
A PACKAGE SENDING SYSTEM?
THE WORLD'S GREATEST SUPER SLIDE.
BUMI, YOU'RE A MAD GENIUS.
HAHAHA! ⚡SNORT⚡

ONE RIDE. THEN WE'RE OFF TO THE NORTH POLE... AIRBENDER'S HONOR.
THIS SOUNDED LIKE FUN AT FIRST, BUT NOW THAT I'M HERE...
I'M STARTING TO HAVE SECOND...
THOUUUUUUGHTS!
YEAAAHHHHHH!
...
???

!!!
I'M ON IT!
AHHHH!
CRUNCH
MEN, YOU'LL BE GOING OFF TO COMBAT SOON. IT'S IMPORTANT THAT YOU BE PREPARED FOR ANYTHING...

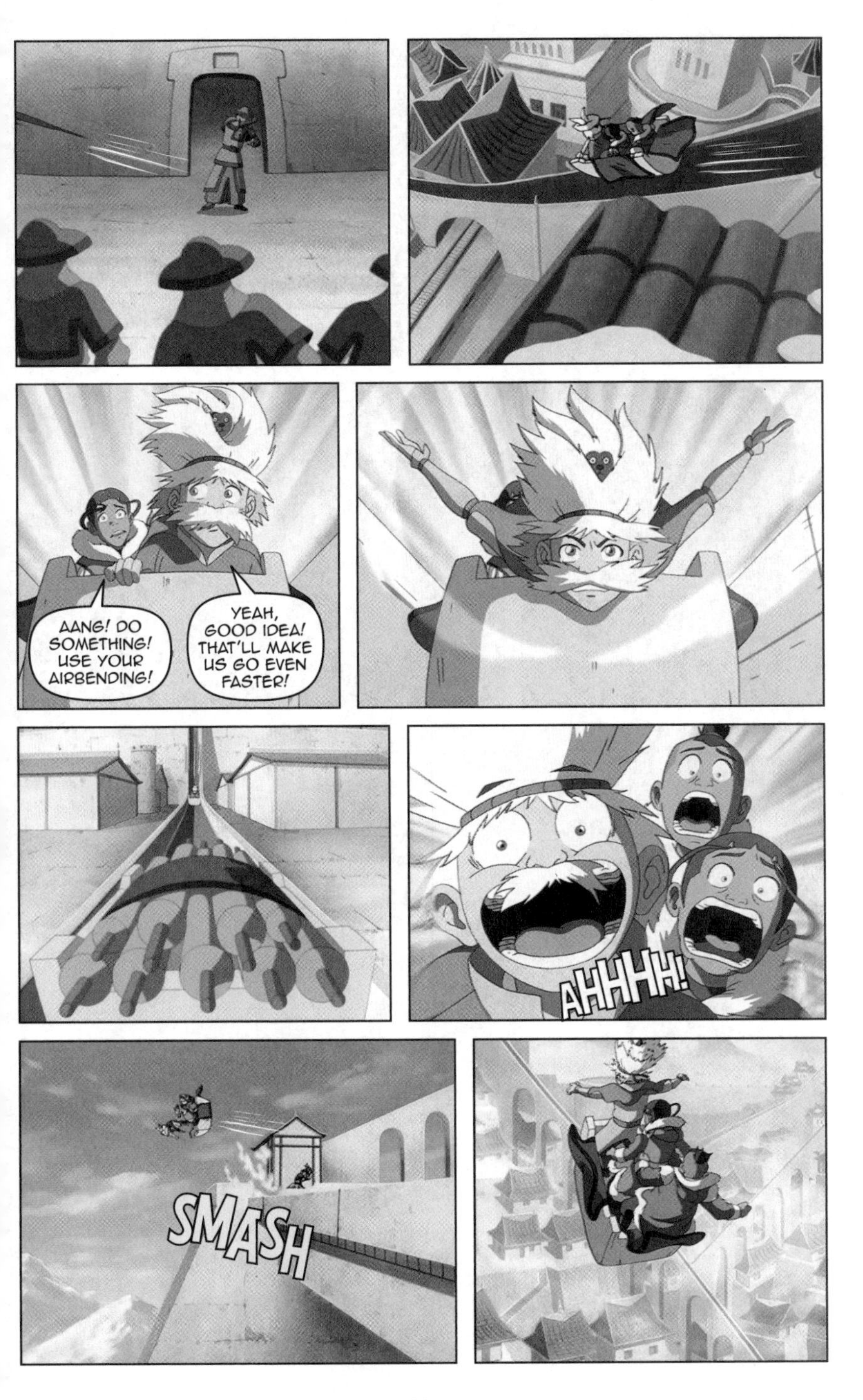
AANG! DO SOMETHING! USE YOUR AIRBENDING!
YEAH, GOOD IDEA! THAT'LL MAKE US GO EVEN FASTER!
AHHHH!
SMASH

CRASH
SORRY!
SMASH
MY CABBAGES! YOU'RE GONNA PAY FOR THIS!
TWO CABBAGES, PLEASE.

KING'S COURT
YOUR MAJESTY, THESE JUVENILES WERE ARRESTED FOR VANDALISM, TRAVELING UNDER FALSE PRETENSES, AND MALICIOUS DESTRUCTION OF CABBAGES.
OFF WITH THEIR HEADS! ONE FOR EACH HEAD OF CABBAGE!
SILENCE! ONLY THE KING CAN PASS DOWN JUDGMENT. WHAT IS YOUR JUDGMENT, SIRE?

THROW THEM...
...A FEAST.

THE PEOPLE IN MY CITY HAVE GOTTEN FAT FROM TOO MANY FEASTS, SO I HOPE YOU LIKE YOUR CHICKEN WITH NO SKIN.
THANKS, BUT I DON'T EAT MEAT.
HOW ABOUT YOU? I BET YOU LIKE MEAT.
MMPPHH!
IS IT JUST ME, OR IS THIS GUY'S CROWN A LITTLE CROOKED?
SO TELL ME, YOUNG BALD ONE, WHERE ARE YOU FROM?
I'M FROM... KANGAROO ISLAND.
OH, KANGAROO ISLAND, EH? I HEAR THAT PLACE IS REALLY HOPPIN'!

HAHAHAHA!
WHAT? IT WAS PRETTY FUNNY.
WELL, ALL THESE GOOD JOKES ARE MAKING ME TIRED. GUESS IT'S TIME TO HIT THE HAY.

GASP
THERE'S AN AIRBENDER IN OUR PRESENCE, AND NOT JUST ANY AIRBENDER: THE AVATAR!
NOW, WHAT DO YOU HAVE TO SAY FOR YOURSELF, MISTER PIPPINPADDLE-OPPSOKOPOLIS?
OKAY, YOU CAUGHT ME, I'M THE AVATAR. DOING MY AVATAR THING, KEEPING THE WORLD SAFE.
EVERYTHING CHECKS OUT, NO FIREBENDERS HERE. SO...GOOD WORK, EVERYBODY.
LOVE EACH OTHER. RESPECT ALL LIFE. AND DON'T RUN WITH YOUR SPEARS. WE'LL SEE YOU NEXT TIME!
CLANK

YOU CAN'T KEEP US HERE. LET US LEAVE!
LETTUCE LEAF?
WE'RE IN SERIOUS TROUBLE. THIS GUY IS NUTS.
TOMORROW, THE AVATAR WILL FACE THREE DEADLY CHALLENGES. BUT FOR NOW, THE GUARDS WILL SHOW YOU TO YOUR CHAMBER.
MY LIEGE, DO YOU MEAN THE GOOD CHAMBER OR THE BAD CHAMBER?
THE NEWLY REFURBISHED CHAMBER.
WAIT, WHICH ONE ARE WE TALKING ABOUT?
THE ONE THAT USED TO BE THE "BAD CHAMBER."
UNTIL THE RECENT REFURBISHING, THAT IS. OF COURSE, WE'VE BEEN CALLING IT THE "NEW CHAMBER," BUT--WE REALLY SHOULD NUMBER THEM, UH...
...TAKE THEM TO THE REFURBISHED CHAMBER THAT WAS ONCE BAD!

RUMBLE
RUMBLE
HE DID SAY IT WAS NEWLY REFURBISHED.
THIS IS A PRISON CELL? BUT IT'S SO NICE.
NICE OR NOT, WE'RE PRISONERS.
I WONDER WHAT THESE CHALLENGES ARE GOING TO BE.
WE'RE NOT STICKING AROUND TO FIND OUT. THERE'S GOT TO BE SOME WAY OUT OF HERE.
THE AIR VENTS!
IF YOU THINK WE'RE GOING TO FIT THROUGH THERE, YOU'RE CRAZIER THAN THAT KING.

WE CAN'T. BUT MOMO CAN.
MOMO, I NEED YOU TO FIND APPA AND BUST US OUT OF HERE.
GO ON, BOY...GET APPA!
UH, HOW WAS APPA SUPPOSED TO SAVE US, ANYWAY?
APPA IS A TEN-TON FLYING BISON. I THINK HE COULD FIGURE SOMETHING OUT.
WELL, NO POINT ARGUING ABOUT IT NOW. GET SOME REST, AANG. LOOKS LIKE YOU'LL NEED IT FOR TOMORROW.

ZZZZZZ
RUMBLE
SOKKA? KATARA?
WHERE ARE MY FRIENDS?
THE KING WILL FREE THEM IF YOU COMPLETE YOUR CHALLENGES.
AND IF I FAIL?
HE DIDN'T SAY. YOUR STAFF, PLEASE.

TESTING CHAMBERS
FIRST, AVATAR, WHAT DO YOU THINK OF MY NEW OUTFIT? I WANT YOUR HONEST OPINION.
I'M WAITING.
I GUESS IT'S FINE.
EXCELLENT! YOU'VE PASSED THE FIRST TEST!

REALLY?
WELL, NOT ONE OF THE DEADLY TESTS. THE REAL CHALLENGES ARE MUCH MORE, UH... CHALLENGING.
I DON'T HAVE TIME FOR YOUR CRAZY GAMES.
GIVE ME MY FRIENDS BACK. WE'RE LEAVING!
OH, I THOUGHT YOU MIGHT REFUSE, SO I WILL GIVE YOUR FRIENDS SOME SPECIAL SOUVENIRS.
"THOSE DELIGHTFUL RINGS..."

CRRRTCHHH
"...ARE MADE OF PURE JENNAMITE, ALSO KNOWN AS CREEPING CRYSTAL.
"IT'S CRYSTAL THAT GROWS REMARKABLY FAST."
BY NIGHTFALL YOUR FRIENDS WILL BE COMPLETELY COVERED IN IT.
TERRIBLE FATE, REALLY. I CAN STOP IT...BUT ONLY IF YOU COOPERATE.
AH! IT'S ALREADY CREEPING!
CRRRTCHHH
I'LL DO WHAT YOU WANT.

HAHAHAHA!
CRRRTCHHH
CRRRTCHHH
IT SEEMS I'VE LOST MY LUNCHBOX KEY AND I'M HUNGRY.
OH, THERE IT IS!
WOULD YOU MIND FETCHING IT FOR ME?

OOH,
CLIMBING THE
LADDER, NO ONE'S
THOUGHT OF THAT
BEFORE.

SPROINGG
SPLASH

WHAM
THAT'S RIGHT, KEEP DIVING HEAD IN, I'M SURE IT'LL WORK EVENTUALLY.
SNAP
ZZZIP

FOOSH
BOING
THERE. ENJOY YOUR LUNCH. I WANT MY FRIENDS BACK NOW.
NOT YET. I NEED HELP WITH ANOTHER MATTER. IT SEEMS I'VE LOST MY PET, FLOPSIE.

OKAY, FOUND HIM.
BRING HIM TO ME. DADDY WANTS A KISS FROM FLOPSIE.
COME HERE, FLOPSIE.
SMASH
FLOPSIE, WAIT! FLOPSIE! FLOPSIE!

HAHAHA

WAIT A MINUTE.
FLOPSIE?
WAG WAG
FLOPSIE!
TWEEEET

AH, THAT'S A GOOD BOY. YES, WHO HAS A SOFT BELLY?
GUYS, ARE YOU OKAY?
OTHER THAN THE CRYSTAL SLOWLY ENCASING MY ENTIRE BODY? DOING GREAT.
CRRRTCHHH
CRRRTCHH
WHAM
COME ON, I'M READY FOR THE NEXT CHALLENGE.
HAHAHA

YOUR FINAL TEST IS A DUEL. AND AS A SPECIAL TREAT, YOU MAY CHOOSE YOUR OPPONENT.
POINT AND CHOOSE.
SO YOU'RE SAYING...WHOEVER I POINT TO...THAT'S THE PERSON I GET TO FIGHT?

CHOOSE WISELY.
I CHOOSE YOU.
WRONG CHOICE.
STOMP

SKID
YOU THOUGHT I WAS A FRAIL OLD MAN, BUT I'M THE MOST POWERFUL EARTHBENDER YOU'LL EVER SEE.
CAN I FIGHT THE GUY WITH THE AX INSTEAD?
THERE ARE NO TAKE-BACKSIES IN MY KINGDOM.
YOU MIGHT NEED THIS.
WHUP
HYARGH!

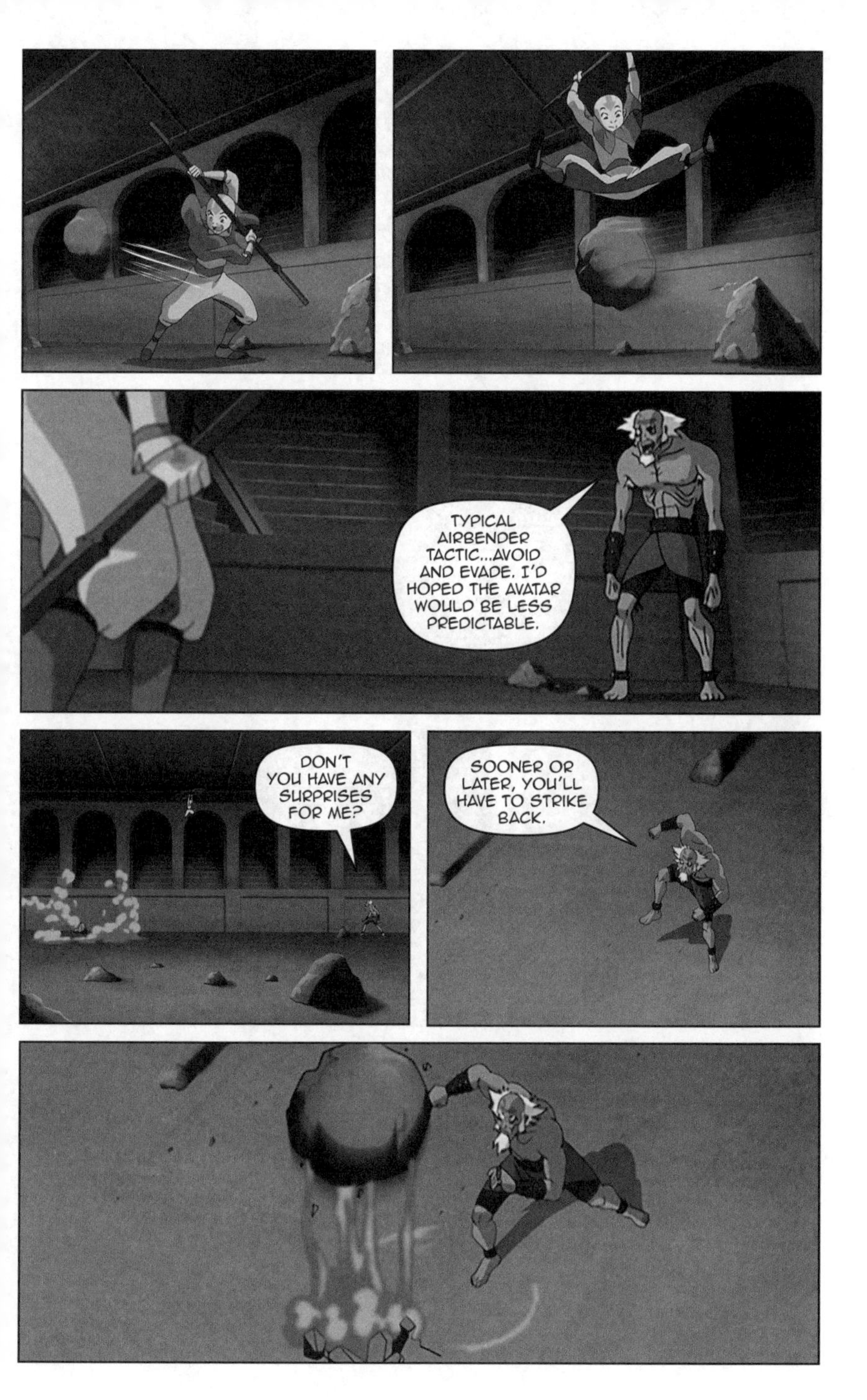
TYPICAL AIRBENDER TACTIC...AVOID AND EVADE. I'D HOPED THE AVATAR WOULD BE LESS PREDICTABLE.
DON'T YOU HAVE ANY SURPRISES FOR ME?
SOONER OR LATER, YOU'LL HAVE TO STRIKE BACK.

SMASH
STOMP
UGH!

OH, YOU'LL HAVE TO BE A LITTLE MORE CREATIVE THAN THAT.

DID SOMEONE LEAVE THE WINDOWS OPEN? IT FEELS A LITTLE DRAFTY IN HERE. ARE YOU HOPING I'LL CATCH A COLD?
RRUMBLE
UGH!

HOW ARE YOU
GOING TO GET ME
FROM WAY OVER
THERE?
OOZE

UGH!
WHAM

CRRAACKKK
WHOOSH
AHHHH!

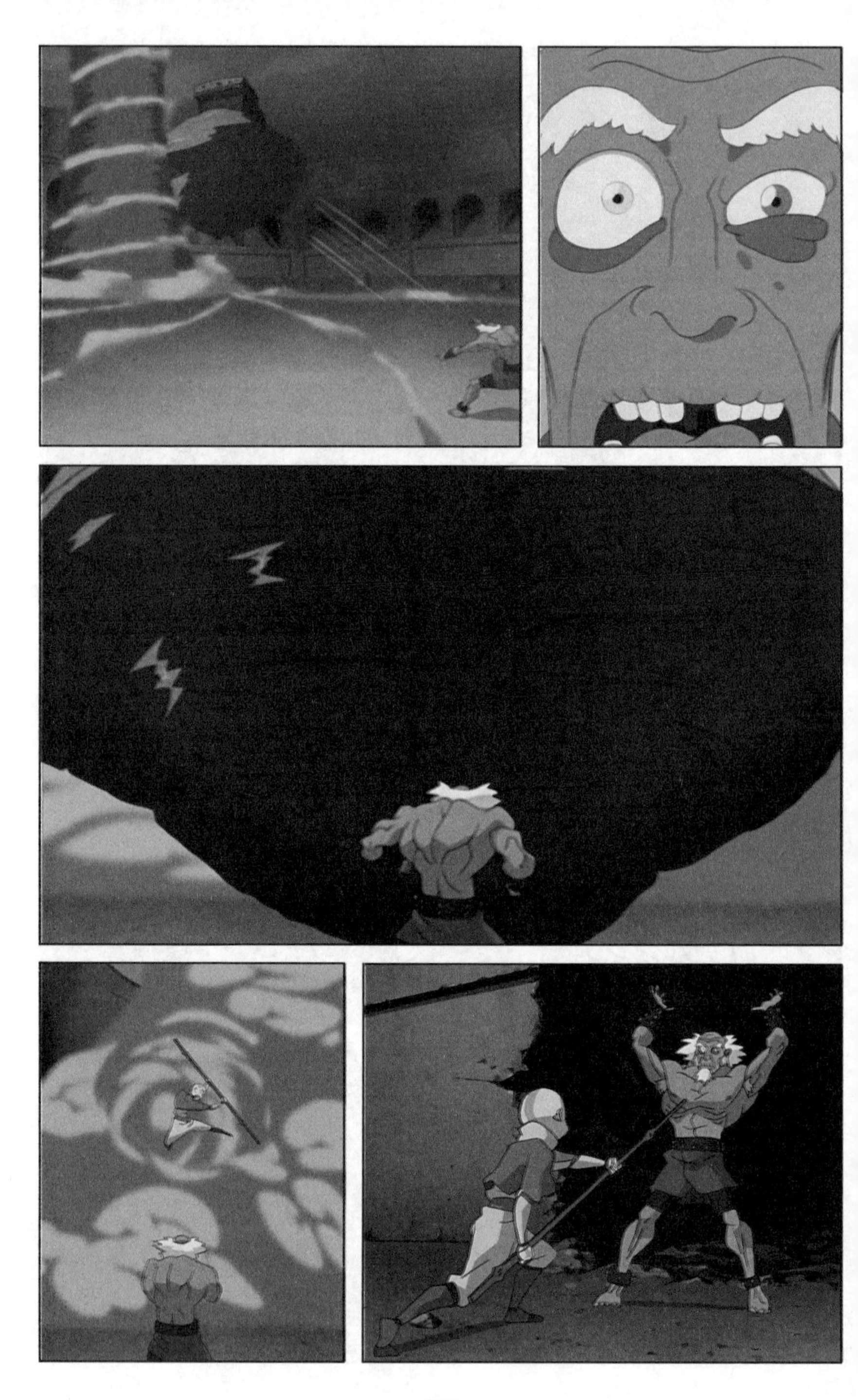

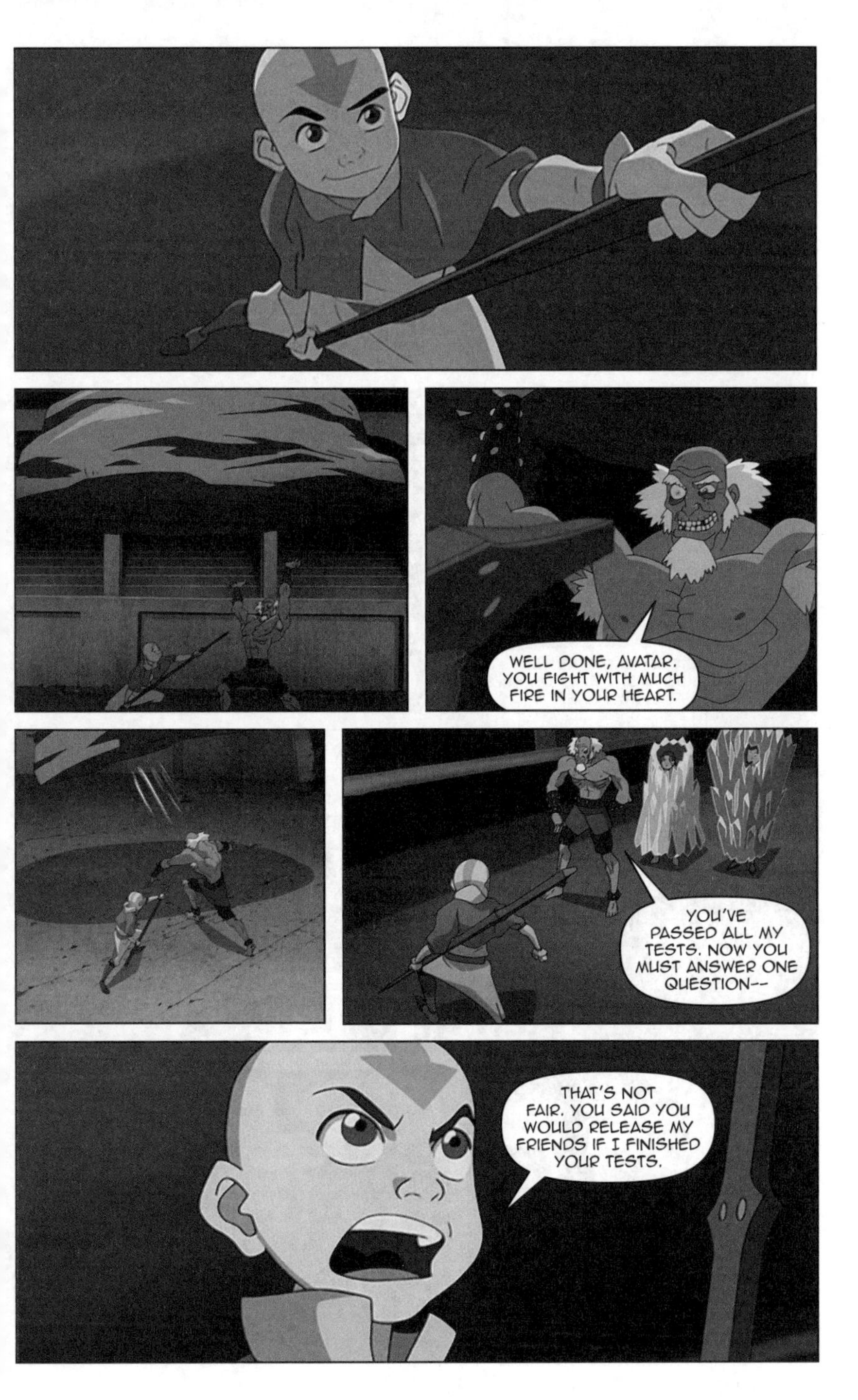
WELL DONE, AVATAR. YOU FIGHT WITH MUCH FIRE IN YOUR HEART.
YOU'VE PASSED ALL MY TESTS. NOW YOU MUST ANSWER ONE QUESTION--
THAT'S NOT FAIR. YOU SAID YOU WOULD RELEASE MY FRIENDS IF I FINISHED YOUR TESTS.

BUT WHAT'S THE POINT OF TESTS IF YOU DON'T LEARN ANYTHING?
OH, COME ON!
ANSWER THIS ONE QUESTION, AND I WILL SET YOUR FRIENDS FREE. WHAT IS MY NAME?
FROM THE LOOKS OF YOUR FRIENDS, I'D SAY YOU ONLY HAVE A FEW MINUTES.
HOW AM I SUPPOSED TO KNOW HIS NAME?
THINK ABOUT THE CHALLENGES. MAYBE IT'S SOME KIND OF RIDDLE--
I GOT IT!
YEAH?
HE'S AN EARTHBENDER, RIGHT?
YOU KNOW, BECAUSE OF ALL THE ROCKS.
ROCKY!

WE'RE GOING TO KEEP TRYING, BUT THAT IS A GOOD BACKUP.
OKAY, SO BACK TO THE CHALLENGES. I GOT A KEY FROM A WATERFALL, I SAVED HIS PET, AND I HAD A DUEL.
AND WHAT DID YOU LEARN?
WELL, EVERYTHING WAS DIFFERENT THAN I EXPECTED.
AND?
WELL, THEY WEREN'T STRAIGHTFORWARD. TO SOLVE EACH TEST, I HAD TO THINK DIFFERENTLY THAN I USUALLY WOULD.
I KNOW HIS NAME.

I SOLVED THE QUESTION THE SAME WAY I SOLVED THE CHALLENGES.
AS YOU SAID A LONG TIME AGO, I HAD TO OPEN MY BRAIN TO THE POSSIBILITIES.
HAHAHA! -SNORT-
BUMI, YOU'RE A MAD GENIUS.
OH, AANG, IT'S GOOD TO SEE YOU. YOU HAVEN'T CHANGED A BIT... LITERALLY.

UH... OVER HERE!
LITTLE HELP?
SMASH
JENNAMITE IS MADE OF ROCK CANDY. DELICIOUS!
SO THIS CRAZY KING...IS YOUR OLD FRIEND BUMI?
WHO YOU CALLING OLD?!

OKAY, I'M OLD.
WHY DID YOU DO ALL THIS, INSTEAD OF JUST TELLING AANG WHO YOU WERE?
FIRST OF ALL, IT'S PRETTY FUN MESSING WITH PEOPLE. BUT I DO HAVE A REASON.
AANG, YOU HAVE A DIFFICULT TASK AHEAD. THE WORLD HAS CHANGED IN THE HUNDRED YEARS YOU'VE BEEN GONE.
IT'S THE DUTY OF THE AVATAR TO RESTORE BALANCE TO THE WORLD BY DEFEATING FIRE LORD OZAI.
YOU HAVE MUCH TO LEARN. YOU MUST MASTER THE FOUR ELEMENTS AND CONFRONT THE FIRE LORD. AND WHEN YOU DO, I HOPE YOU WILL THINK LIKE A MAD GENIUS.

AND IT LOOKS LIKE YOU'RE IN GOOD HANDS. YOU'LL NEED YOUR FRIENDS TO HELP YOU DEFEAT THE FIRE NATION.
AND YOU'LL NEED MOMO, TOO!
THANK YOU FOR YOUR WISDOM. BUT BEFORE WE LEAVE, I HAVE A CHALLENGE FOR YOU...

AHHH!
WOOHOO!
CRASH
MY CABBAGES!

CHAPTER SIX

IMPRISONED

EARTH NATION
GREAT, YOU'RE BACK. WHAT'S FOR DINNER?
WE'VE GOT A FEW OPTIONS.
FIRST, ROUND NUTS. AND SOME KIND OF OVAL-SHAPED NUTS. AND SOME ROCK-SHAPED NUTS...THAT MIGHT JUST BE ROCKS.
DIG IN.
SERIOUSLY, WHAT ELSE YOU GOT?
BOOM
WHAT WAS THAT?
IT'S COMING FROM OVER THERE!
SHOULDN'T WE RUN AWAY FROM HUGE BOOMS, NOT TOWARD THEM?

WHAM
AN EARTHBENDER.
LET'S GO MEET HIM.
HE LOOKS DANGEROUS, SO WE BETTER APPROACH CAUTIOUSLY.
HELLO THERE! I'M KATARA. WHAT'S YOUR NAME?

CRASH
NICE TO MEET YOU!
I JUST WANTED TO SAY HI.
HEY, THAT GUY'S GOTTA BE RUNNING SOMEWHERE--MAYBE WE'RE NEAR A VILLAGE...
AND I BET THAT VILLAGE HAS A MARKET!
WHICH MEANS NO NUTS FOR DINNER!
CHIRP
HEY, I WORKED HARD TO GET THOSE NUTS!
NAH. I HATE 'EM, TOO.

GREAT HAT! I'LL TRADE YOU SOME NUTS FOR IT.
HEY.
HI, MOM.
WHERE HAVE YOU BEEN, HARU? YOU'RE LATE. GET STARTED ON YOUR CHORES.
HEY, YOU'RE THAT KID. WHY DID YOU RUN AWAY BEFORE?
UH, YOU MUST HAVE ME CONFUSED WITH SOME OTHER KID.

NO, SHE DOESN'T. WE SAW YOU EARTHBENDING.
GASP
THEY SAW YOU DOING WHAT?
THEY'RE CRAZY, MOM! I MEAN, LOOK AT HOW THEY'RE DRESSED.
YOU KNOW HOW DANGEROUS THAT IS! YOU KNOW WHAT WOULD HAPPEN IF THEY CAUGHT YOU EARTHBENDING!
BANG
BANG
OPEN UP!

FIRE NATION!
ACT NATURAL!
...
WHAT DO YOU WANT?
I'VE ALREADY PAID
YOU THIS WEEK.
THE TAX JUST DOUBLED.
AND WE WOULDN'T WANT
AN ACCIDENT, WOULD WE?
FIRE--IT'S SOMETIMES
SO HARD TO CONTROL.

YOU CAN KEEP THE COPPER ONES.
NICE GUY. HOW LONG HAS THE FIRE NATION BEEN HERE?
FIVE YEARS. FIRE LORD OZAI USES OUR TOWN'S COAL MINES TO FUEL HIS SHIPS.
THEY'RE THUGS. THEY STEAL FROM US. AND EVERYONE HERE IS TOO MUCH OF A COWARD TO DO ANYTHING ABOUT IT.
QUIET, HARU. DON'T TALK LIKE THAT.

BUT HARU'S AN EARTHBENDER. HE CAN HELP!
EARTHBENDING IS FORBIDDEN. IT'S CAUSED NOTHING BUT MISERY FOR THIS VILLAGE. HE MUST NEVER USE HIS ABILITIES.
HOW CAN YOU SAY THAT? HARU HAS A GIFT! ASKING HIM NOT TO EARTHBEND IS LIKE ASKING ME NOT TO WATERBEND. IT'S A PART OF WHO WE ARE.
YOU DON'T UNDERSTAND.
I UNDERSTAND THAT HARU CAN HELP YOU FIGHT BACK. WHAT CAN THE FIRE NATION DO TO YOU THAT THEY HAVEN'T DONE ALREADY?
THEY COULD TAKE HARU AWAY. LIKE THEY TOOK HIS FATHER.

MY MOM SAID YOU CAN SLEEP HERE TONIGHT. BUT YOU SHOULD LEAVE IN THE MORNING.
THANKS. I'LL MAKE SURE APPA DOESN'T EAT ALL YOUR HAY.
MUNCH MUNCH
I'M SORRY ABOUT WHAT I SAID EARLIER. I DIDN'T KNOW ABOUT YOUR FATHER.
THAT'S OKAY. IT'S FUNNY, THE WAY YOU WERE TALKING BACK IN THE STORE--IT REMINDED ME OF HIM.
THANKS.
MY FATHER WAS VERY COURAGEOUS. WHEN THE FIRE NATION INVADED, HE AND THE OTHER EARTHBENDERS WERE OUTNUMBERED TEN TO ONE, BUT THEY FOUGHT BACK ANYWAY.
HE SOUNDS LIKE A GREAT MAN.

AFTER THE ATTACK, THEY ROUNDED UP MY FATHER AND EVERY OTHER EARTHBENDER, AND TOOK THEM AWAY. WE HAVEN'T SEEN THEM SINCE.
SO THAT'S WHY YOU HIDE YOUR EARTHBENDING.
YEAH.
THE PROBLEM IS...THE ONLY WAY I CAN FEEL CLOSE TO MY FATHER NOW IS WHEN I PRACTICE MY BENDING.
HE TAUGHT ME EVERYTHING I KNOW.
SEE THIS NECKLACE?
MY MOTHER GAVE IT TO ME.
IT'S BEAUTIFUL.
I LOST MY MOTHER IN A FIRE NATION RAID. THIS NECKLACE IS ALL I HAVE LEFT OF HER.
IT'S NOT ENOUGH, IS IT?
NO.

BOOM
THE MINE!
HELP!
RUMBLE
HELP ME!
IT'S NOT WORKING. WE HAVE TO GET HELP!
THERE'S NO TIME. PULL HARDER!
HARU, THERE'S A WAY YOU CAN HELP HIM!
I CAN'T.
RUMBLE
RUMBLE
PLEASE, THERE'S NO ONE AROUND TO SEE YOU. IT'S THE ONLY WAY!
RRUMBLE
RRUMBLE

WHOOSH
HARU!
YOU DID IT!

IT WAS SO BRAVE OF HARU TO USE HIS EARTHBENDING TO HELP THAT OLD MAN.
YOU MUST HAVE REALLY INSPIRED HIM.
I GUESS SO.
EVERYONE SHOULD GET SOME SLEEP. WE'RE LEAVING AT DAWN.
DAWN? CAN'T WE SLEEP IN FOR ONCE?
ABSOLUTELY NOT. THIS VILLAGE IS CRAWLING WITH FIRE NATION TROOPS. IF THEY DISCOVER YOU'RE HERE, AANG, WE'LL BE EATING FIREBALLS FOR BREAKFAST.
GOOD NIGHT.
I'D RATHER EAT FIREBALLS THAN NUTS.
GOOD NIGHT!
HEHEHE!

HARU'S HOME
BANG
BANG
BANG
GASP
THAT'S HIM.
THAT'S THE EARTHBENDER.

THEY TOOK HIM. THEY TOOK HARU AWAY.
WHAT?
THE OLD MAN TURNED HIM IN TO THE FIRE NATION. IT'S ALL MY FAULT. I FORCED HIM INTO EARTHBENDING.
SLOW DOWN, KATARA. WHEN DID THIS HAPPEN?
HARU'S MOTHER SAID THEY CAME FOR HIM AT MIDNIGHT.
THEN IT'S TOO LATE TO TRACK HIM. HE'S LONG GONE.
WE DON'T NEED TO TRACK HIM. THE FIRE NATION IS GOING TO TAKE ME RIGHT TO HARU.
AND WHY WOULD THEY DO THAT?
BECAUSE THEY'RE GOING TO ARREST ME FOR EARTHBENDING.

MINE ENTRANCE
I THOUGHT YOU WERE CRAZY AT FIRST, KATARA, BUT THIS MIGHT WORK.
THERE ARE VENTILATION SHAFTS THROUGHOUT THESE MINES.
ALL AANG HAS TO DO IS SEND AN AIR CURRENT FROM THAT VENT TO THIS ONE RIGHT HERE. THE BOULDER LEVITATES AND...TAH-DAH!
FAKE EARTHBENDING.
AANG, DID YOU GET ALL THAT?
SURE, SURE. I GOT IT.
DO YOU REMEMBER YOUR CUE?
YEAH, YEAH, JUST RELAX. YOU'RE TAKING ALL THE FUN OUT OF THIS.
BY "THIS," DO YOU MEAN INTENTIONALLY BEING CAPTURED BY AN ARMY OF RUTHLESS FIREBENDERS?

EXACTLY. THAT'S FUN STUFF!
HERE THEY COME. GET IN YOUR PLACES.
GET OUT OF MY WAY, PIPSQUEAK!
HOW DARE YOU CALL ME PIPSQUEAK, YOU GIANT-EARED CRETIN!
WHAT DID YOU CALL ME?
A GIANT-EARED CRETIN! LOOK AT THOSE THINGS. DO HERDS OF ANIMALS USE THEM FOR SHADE?
YOU BETTER BACK OFF!
SERIOUSLY, BACK OFF.

I WILL NOT BACK OFF! I BET ELEPHANTS GET TOGETHER AND MAKE FUN OF HOW LARGE YOUR EARS ARE.
THAT'S IT! YOU'RE GOING DOWN!
I'LL SHOW YOU WHO'S BOSS!
EARTHBENDING STYLE!
I SAID, EARTHBENDING STYLE!
WHOOSH

THAT LEMUR--HE'S EARTHBENDING!
NO, YOU IDIOT. IT'S THE GIRL!

OH... OF COURSE.
I'LL HOLD HER!
YOU'VE GOT TWELVE HOURS TO FIND HARU. WE'LL BE RIGHT BEHIND YOU.
MOMO, YOU HAVE SOME BIG EARS.

SHE'LL BE FINE, AANG. KATARA KNOWS WHAT SHE'S DOING.

OFFSHORE PRISON RIG
EARTHBENDERS, IT IS MY PLEASURE TO WELCOME YOU ABOARD MY MODEST SHIPYARD.
I AM YOUR WARDEN. I PREFER TO THINK OF YOU NOT AS PRISONERS BUT AS HONORED GUESTS...
AND I HOPE YOU COME TO THINK OF ME AS YOUR HUMBLE AND CARING HOST.
YOU WILL SUCCEED HERE IF YOU SIMPLY ABIDE--
COUGH
FWOOSH
WHAT KIND OF GUEST DISHONORS HIS HOST BY INTERRUPTING HIM?

TAKE HIM BELOW. ONE WEEK IN SOLITARY WILL IMPROVE HIS MANNERS.
SIMPLY TREAT ME WITH THE COURTESY I GIVE YOU AND WE'LL GET ALONG FAMOUSLY.
"YOU WILL NOTICE, EARTHBENDERS, THAT THIS RIG IS MADE ENTIRELY OF METAL.
"YOU ARE MILES AWAY FROM ANY ROCK OR EARTH.
"SO IF YOU HAVE ANY ILLUSIONS ABOUT EMPLOYING THAT BRUTISH SAVAGERY THAT PASSES FOR BENDING AMONG YOU PEOPLE...
"...FORGET THEM.
"IT IS IMPOSSIBLE."
GOOD DAY.

KATARA?
HARU!
WHAT ARE YOU DOING HERE?
IT'S MY FAULT YOU WERE CAPTURED. I CAME TO RESCUE YOU.
SO YOU GOT YOURSELF ARRESTED?
IT WAS THE ONLY WAY TO FIND YOU.
YOU'VE GOT GUTS, KATARA, I'LL GIVE YOU THAT. COME ON, THERE'S SOMEONE I WANT YOU TO MEET.

KATARA, THIS IS MY FATHER, TYRO.
DAD, THIS IS KATARA.
IT'S AN HONOR TO MEET YOU.
HAVE SOME DINNER, KATARA.
EWWW.
IT'S NOT AS BAD AS IT LOOKS. IT'S STILL PRETTY BAD, THOUGH.
TYRO, THE PRISONERS ARE COMPLAINING THERE AREN'T ENOUGH BLANKETS TO GO AROUND.

I'LL TALK TO THE GUARDS. IN THE MEANTIME, MAKE SURE THE ELDERLY ARE TAKEN CARE OF. THE REST OF US WILL SIMPLY HAVE TO HOPE FOR WARMER WEATHER.
IF YOU DON'T MIND ME ASKING, WHAT'S YOUR ESCAPE PLAN?
EXCUSE ME?
YOU KNOW, THE PLAN TO GET EVERYONE OFF THE RIG. WHAT IS IT, MUTINY? SABOTAGE?
THE PLAN? THE PLAN IS TO SURVIVE. WAIT OUT THIS WAR. HOPE THAT ONE DAY SOME OF US CAN GET BACK HOME AND FORGET THIS EVER HAPPENED.
HOW CAN YOU SAY THAT? YOU SOUND LIKE YOU'VE ALREADY GIVEN UP.

KATARA, I ADMIRE YOUR COURAGE. AND I ENVY YOUR YOUTH. BUT PEOPLE'S LIVES ARE AT STAKE HERE.
THE WARDEN IS A RUTHLESS MAN, AND HE WON'T STAND FOR ANY REBELLION. I'M SORRY, BUT WE'RE POWERLESS.
WE'LL SEE ABOUT THAT.
TINK TINK
EARTHBENDERS, YOU DON'T KNOW ME, BUT I KNOW OF YOU.
EVERY CHILD IN MY WATER TRIBE VILLAGE WAS ROCKED TO SLEEP WITH STORIES OF THE BRAVE EARTH KINGDOM AND THE COURAGEOUS EARTHBENDERS WHO GUARD ITS BORDERS.
SOME OF YOU MAY THINK THAT THE FIRE NATION HAS MADE YOU POWERLESS.

YES, THEY HAVE TAKEN AWAY YOUR ABILITY TO BEND. BUT THEY CAN'T TAKE AWAY YOUR COURAGE. AND IT IS YOUR COURAGE THEY SHOULD TRULY FEAR...
BECAUSE IT RUNS DEEPER THAN ANY MINE YOU'VE BEEN FORCED TO DIG, ANY OCEAN THAT KEEPS YOU FAR FROM HOME.
IT IS THE STRENGTH OF YOUR HEARTS THAT MAKE YOU WHO YOU ARE, HEARTS THAT WILL REMAIN UNBROKEN WHEN ALL ROCK AND STONE HAS ERODED AWAY.
THE TIME TO FIGHT BACK IS NOW. I CAN TELL YOU, THE AVATAR HAS RETURNED! SO REMEMBER YOUR COURAGE, EARTHBENDERS.

LET US FIGHT FOR OUR FREEDOM!

YOUR TWELVE HOURS ARE UP. WHERE'S HARU? WE'VE GOT TO GET OUT OF HERE.
I CAN'T.
WE DON'T HAVE MUCH TIME. THERE ARE GUARDS EVERYWHERE. GET ON!
KATARA, WHAT'S WRONG?
I'M NOT LEAVING. I'M NOT GIVING UP ON THESE PEOPLE.

WHAT DO YOU MEAN YOU'RE NOT LEAVING?
WE CAN'T ABANDON THESE PEOPLE. THERE HAS TO BE A WAY TO HELP THEM!
MAYBE SHE'S RIGHT. WHAT DO YOU SAY, SOKKA?
I SAY YOU'RE BOTH CRAZY.
LAST CHANCE. WE NEED TO LEAVE. NOW!
NO.
I HATE WHEN YOU GET LIKE THIS. COME ON, WE BETTER HIDE.
PSSS PSS PSS PSSS.
LOOK!

SOON...
TELL ME EXACTLY WHAT YOU SAW.
WELL, SIR, IT LOOKED LIKE A FLYING BISON.
WHAT?
IT WAS A GIANT FLYING BUFFALO, SIR. WITH AN EMPTY SADDLE.
WHICH WAS IT? A BUFFALO OR A BISON?
I'M NOT SURE WHAT THE DIFFERENCE IS. BUT THAT'S NOT REALLY THE POINT, IS IT, SIR?

I'LL DECIDE WHAT THE POINT IS, FOOL!
AAAAAHHHHH!
YOU. WAKE UP THE CAPTAIN. SEARCH THE ENTIRE RIG.
SIR?
WHAT?
THAT WAS THE CAPTAIN YOU JUST THREW OVERBOARD. SO...
THEN WAKE UP SOMEONE I HAVEN'T THROWN OVERBOARD AND SEARCH THE RIG.
THERE'S SOMETHING GOING ON HERE, AND I DON'T LIKE IT.

WE DON'T HAVE MUCH TIME. WHAT ARE WE GOING TO DO?
I WISH I KNEW HOW TO MAKE A HURRICANE.
THE WARDEN WOULD RUN AWAY AND WE'D STEAL HIS KEYS.
WOULDN'T HE JUST TAKE HIS KEYS WITH HIM?
I'M JUST TOSSING IDEAS AROUND.

I TRIED TALKING THE EARTHBENDERS INTO FIGHTING BACK, BUT IT DIDN'T WORK.
IF THERE WAS JUST A WAY TO HELP THEM HELP THEMSELVES.
FOR THAT THEY'D NEED SOME EARTH OR SOME ROCK. SOMETHING THEY CAN BEND...
BUT THIS ENTIRE PLACE IS MADE OF METAL.
NO, IT'S NOT. LOOK AT THE SMOKE.
I BET THEY'RE BURNING COAL.
IN OTHER WORDS...EARTH.

IT'S ALMOST DAWN. WE'RE RUNNING OUT OF TIME. YOU SURE THIS IS GOING TO WORK?
IT SHOULD.
THESE VENTS REMINDED ME OF OUR LITTLE TRICK BACK AT THE VILLAGE. WE'RE GOING TO DO THE SAME THING, BUT ON A MUCH BIGGER SCALE.
THERE'S A HUGE DEPOSIT OF COAL AT THE BASE OF THE SILO. AND THE WHOLE SYSTEM IS VENTILATED. AANG CLOSED OFF ALL THE VENTS...
EXCEPT ONE.

WHEN HE DOES HIS AIRBENDING, THE COAL ONLY HAS ONE PLACE TO GO...RIGHT BACK HERE.
THERE'S THE INTRUDER!
STAY BACK! I'M WARNING YOU!
KATARA, STOP! YOU CAN'T WIN THIS FIGHT.
LISTEN TO HIM WELL, CHILD. YOU'RE ONE MISTAKE AWAY FROM DYING WHERE YOU STAND.

RRUMMBLE
RRUMBLE
BOOOM

≈COUGH≈
HERE'S YOUR CHANCE, EARTHBENDERS. TAKE IT! YOUR FATE IS IN YOUR OWN HANDS.
HAHAHAHA!
FOOLISH GIRL, YOU THOUGHT A FEW INSPIRATIONAL WORDS AND SOME COAL WOULD CHANGE THESE PEOPLE?
LOOK AT THESE BLANK, HOPELESS FACES. THEIR SPIRITS WERE BROKEN A LONG TIME AGO.

OH, BUT YOU STILL BELIEVE IN THEM? HOW SWEET. THEY'RE A WASTE OF YOUR ENERGY, LITTLE GIRL.
YOU'VE FAILED.
BONK
WHUP
WHUP

FWOOSH
THUK
SHOW NO MERCY!

FOR THE EARTH KINGDOM!
ATTACK!

THWACK
SMASH

GET TO THE SHIP! WE'LL HOLD THEM OFF!
DO NOT LET THEM ESCAPE!
GUYS, THROW ME SOME COAL!

THWACK
THWACK
THWACK

NO! PLEASE!
I CAN'T SWIM!
DON'T WORRY,
I HEAR COWARDS
FLOAT.
AHHHHH!

I WANT TO THANK YOU FOR SAVING ME. FOR SAVING US.
ALL IT TOOK WAS A LITTLE COAL.
IT WASN'T THE COAL, KATARA. IT WAS YOU.
THANK YOU FOR HELPING ME FIND MY COURAGE, KATARA OF THE WATER TRIBE. MY FAMILY--AND EVERYONE HERE--OWES YOU MUCH.
SO I GUESS YOU'RE GOING HOME NOW.
YES. TO TAKE BACK MY VILLAGE.
TO TAKE BACK ALL OF OUR VILLAGES! THE FIRE NATION WILL REGRET THE DAY THEY SET FOOT ON OUR LAND!

HOORAY
COME WITH US.
I CAN'T.
YOUR MISSION IS TO TAKE BACK YOUR HOME. OURS IS TO GET AANG TO THE NORTH POLE.
THAT'S HIM, ISN'T IT? THE AVATAR.
KATARA, THANK YOU FOR BRINGING MY FATHER BACK TO ME. I NEVER THOUGHT I'D SEE HIM AGAIN. I ONLY WISH THERE WAS SOME WAY...
I KNOW.
MY MOTHER'S NECKLACE. IT'S GONE.

CREDITS

CHAPTER ONE
THE BOY IN THE ICEBERG

WRITTEN BY MICHAEL DANTE DIMARTINO
BRYAN KONIETZKO

ADDITIONAL WRITING BY
AARON EHASZ
PETER GOLDFINGER
JOSH STOLBERG

DIRECTED BY DAVE FILONI

ASSISTANT DIRECTED BY
JUSTIN RIDGE
GIANCARLO VOLPE

CO-PRODUCER: AARON EHASZ

CHAPTER TWO
THE AVATAR RETURNS

WRITTEN BY MICHAEL DANTE DIMARTINO
BRYAN KONIETZKO

ADDITIONAL WRITING BY
AARON EHASZ
PETER GOLDFINGER
JOSH STOLBERG

DIRECTED BY DAVE FILONI

ASSISTANT DIRECTED BY
JUSTIN RIDGE
MIYUKI HOSHIKAWA

CO-PRODUCER: AARON EHASZ

CHAPTER THREE
THE SOUTHERN AIR TEMPLE

WRITTEN BY MICHAEL DANTE DIMARTINO

HEAD WRITER
AARON EHASZ

DIRECTED BY LAUREN MACMULLAN

ASSISTANT DIRECTED BY
LI HONG
ETHAN SPAULDING

CO-PRODUCER: AARON EHASZ

CHAPTER FOUR
THE WARRIORS OF KYOSHI

WRITTEN BY NICK MALIS

HEAD WRITER
AARON EHASZ

DIRECTED BY GIANCARLO VOLPE

ASSISTANT DIRECTED BY
CHRIS GRAHAM
KENJI ONO

CO-PRODUCER: AARON EHASZ

CHAPTER FIVE
THE KING OF OMASHU

WRITTEN BY JOHN O'BRYAN

HEAD WRITER
AARON EHASZ

DIRECTED BY ANTHONY LIOI

ASSISTANT DIRECTED BY
IAN GRAHAM
BOBBY RUBIO

CO-PRODUCER: AARON EHASZ

CHAPTER SIX
IMPRISONED

WRITTEN BY MATTHEW HUBBARD

HEAD WRITER
AARON EHASZ

DIRECTED BY DAVE FILONI

ASSISTANT DIRECTED BY
MIYUKI HOSHIKAWA
JUSTIN RIDGE

PRODUCER: AARON EHASZ

EXECUTIVE PRODUCERS: MICHAEL DANTE DIMARTINO & BRYAN KONIETZKO